HOUSE OF THE MOON QUEEN

By the same author

Comics featuring the Moon Queen

GOLDEN TABLES OF THE WORLD

THE HORROR OF SECTION 4

TORUS

Other comics

THE NEW WORLD: COMICS FROM MAURETANIA

CODEWORD: CRIME

CINEMA DETECTIVES THE UNEXPECTED

FUTURE FARM STORIES

JENNY IN STRINGTOWN

Photo comics

PROWL CAR

PROWL CAR: POWER AND CONTROL

PROWL CAR: SECRET AGENTS

PROWL CAR D.M.I.C. DELHI-MUMBAI INDUSTRIAL CORRIDOR
GHOST SHIP

PROWL CAR ACADEMY

PROWL CAR KUALA LUMPUR: PROWL CAR INTERNATIONAL

Prose stories

LAST COP AT ROSEISLE

CELLARHEAD

HOUSE OF THE MOON QUEEN

Chris Reynolds

Edited by Kevin Walker

walker.kevin.william@gmail.com

busyguessing.wordpress.com

ISBN:9798449393302

cinemadetectives.com

Chapter One

The Young Master chuckled with excitement as he slipped away from the breakfast table. He peered along the passage that led towards the playroom, where robot AM-10 would already be laying out the trains, but he did not go that way. Instead, he opened the seldom-used door that led to the older part of the house. It unlatched easily, and he slipped through, feeling a thrill of excitement as he set out on his secret expedition. Sunlight from the high windows gleamed on his golden hair as he hurried along, enjoying the slap of his footsteps on the bare stone floors and the flicker and rustle of summer leaves from outside. He thought of AM-10, diligently at work assembling the railway, and grinned. Playing trains usually took them until lunch, and then after lunch there would be games outside in the grounds, but today the Young Master wanted to do something different. The boy thought of the room he had seen during yesterday's hide-and-seek, and as he hurried along he felt as if he was playing hide-and-seek again, except that this time AM-10 was unaware of the game.

He slowed down at the large scary room full of ancient, cruel-looking hunting equipment, walking the length of it cautiously, before coming to the foot of a broad flight of stairs. Here he paused, as he had done when he had come this way before, because around the walls of the stairwell stood several huge silver statues of women. The Young Master knew that these were robots, but of a different kind to AM-10 and the rest who looked after him. These merely stood there in silence, as if listening to everything that went on in the house. As he crept up the stairs, the Young Master glanced at the reflection of his face in their shining bodies.

'I'm only playing a game,' he whispered guiltily, but the silver women, as ever, made no response. At the top of the stairs, he ran along another corridor. Not far now. He sprinted towards the special room and turned the door handle.

The place looked just as mysterious as before. Just enough light came through the leaded windows for him to see some chairs, a table, and rows and rows of glass-fronted cupboards. But the things he had seen inside the cupboards were what excited him most - rows of flat black things with gold markings. From his glimpse of this room yesterday, the Young Master had felt he almost remembered them, as if from a dream. The glass door of the cupboard rattled slightly as he tugged at the little handle. Then he reached inside to draw out one of the flat things. He lifted it down and carried it across to the table, where he opened it up, and then gaped in amazement. It was full of papers, all gathered together at one side, and covered in markings. This was so exciting! Why had AM-10 never brought him to this room? As the Young Master turned page after page, the words in the book reflected back across his eyes, but he could not read, and so the words did not have the power to unlock his thoughts or memories.

He turned at the slight sound of another robot entering the room. It was U-3. The U-series robots never spoke, although they could contact AM-10, even from a distance. A faint clicking came from U-3's head. The Young

Master knew that it was in touch with AM-10 now, and he knew that this game was over. AM-10 would already be hurrying through the corridors to collect him.

Sure enough, just a few minutes later, the robot arrived. 'It is not often we find you in the Library, Sir,' AM-10 said as he stood in the doorway.

'No, AM-10. But look what I've found!' The Young Master eagerly showed the robot the book. 'See the little shapes? There are just a few kinds of them, but they're repeated over and over again, all in different combinations.'

'A most intriguing discovery, Sir,' AM-10 replied coolly. 'But now surely it is time to run the trains?'

The Young Master nodded happily and, leaving the book on the table, followed AM-10 out from the room. U-3 remained behind.

'I have assembled a very large railway for us, Sir,' AM-10 said and went on to describe the double track, the stations, and the bridges he had built, but as he spoke his head made the clicking noise that meant he was contacting another robot.

'AM-10 ---> U-3 : Thank you for alerting me to the Young Master's presence in the Library.'

'U-3 ---> AM-10: He had not been in that room for long. Shall I destroy the books?'

'AM-10 ---> U-3 : Destruction remains unnecessary, but please inform me immediately if the Young Master ever returns to the Library again.'

Chapter Two

The taxi drove up the hill.

'I remember coming up here as a kid,' the cab driver said. 'All the houses here had already been taken by the old Superheroes even then. They all wanted to live here. Me and the other kids, we used to go exploring. We'd climb the trees and watch while they had their alterations made to each house. If they saw you, they'd chase you away. One kid, they almost killed him when he got too interested, so then we didn't come this way very much anymore. Which one did you say you were going to?'

'Crystal House,' Louise Bale replied. 'But I don't know where it is or what it looks like because I've never been here before.'

'So how come you're visiting one of the old Superheroes? There are hardly any of them left alive now. They're all slowly dying off, one by one.'

'That's right. My aunt was Agnes Bale, and she's just recently died. That's why I've come. She's left me the house we're going to - Crystal House.'

'I'm sorry.'

'That's OK. I never knew her.'

'She was one of them, wasn't she? She was the one they used to call the *Moon Queen*.'

The taxi drove on up the hill among the towering trees.

'I never even knew about her before she died,' Louise said. 'I never really thought about the Superheroes at all until I got the letter saying I'd inherited the house. I still don't properly know who my aunt was or what she did.'

'I remember some about her, Ma'am. I used to have all the comics. I used to like the pictures of them all flying through the air and of their fights. Battles with *Supervillains*. Were you interested in those fights? I suppose not.'

'No. But I have seen a fight.' It was difficult for Louise to keep it in. *Just say the words*, she thought to herself, *tell people often enough and I might get it all out of my head*. 'It wasn't a Superhero who was in this particular fight - it was me.'

The driver looked at Louise in the mirror as he caught the edge of fear in her voice.

'I have to tell people about it sometimes,' Louise said, 'because I'm still trying to make sense of it myself.'

In the mirror, the taxi man's face looked worried. He tried to change the subject by repeating something he'd heard on the news about President Rayonier's grab for the southern Oil Lands, but it was as if Louise never heard him.

'I had a boyfriend called Jeff,' she said. 'Jeff Butler. He loved the Superheroes and he knew all about them.'

'Go on,' the taxi driver said, resigned, turning the wheel on a sharp turn. The cab was old and did not have power steering.

'Jeff was actually writing a book about the Superheroes, and he had just been in touch with one of them called Conway Johns. Johns used to be *T-Man*, and Jeff said he was probably the most famous of them all. Jeff was so pleased to make contact with him.'

'I know about T-Man. Good ol' *Cup-of-Tea Man.* Got his autograph as a kid,' the taxi driver enthused, still trying to change the direction of the conversation.

'I never met Johns myself, but Jeff corresponded with him for a few weeks, and then one day Jeff was invited over to the house where Johns lived. He was excited, like a little kid.'

'Conway Johns never had any of the houses up here,' the taxi driver said. 'He never had a house on this hill. Nor anywhere else in Crescent City. He always lived in his own town, Steel Ring City.'

'That's right, Steel Ring City, that's where I come from. I'd thought things were going well between me and Jeff. Jeff was nice but he was always into this Superhero thing. He was so interested in them.

'I was waiting at home for him. When he got back from seeing T-Man I was going to make him dinner and let him tell me all about it. But he came back early. It was a long time before we were meant to have the food.' Louise stopped. The taxi man checked her in the mirror and saw tears in her eyes.

'I'll stop the car if you need some air. Don't worry, I'll stop the meter.'

'No, that's OK.' Louise touched the solid bodywork of the car, as if she was more comfortable in motion, as if she had to keep running.

'I started making the food. I was by the stove, and I was talking to Jeff, calling through to him in the next room, but he didn't answer. So I began to get a bit annoyed. And then suddenly he was in the kitchen with me, and he was angry too. Something had gone wrong with his visit to Conway Johns. I hadn't noticed. Then he started yelling, telling me that I was stupid, as if it was all my fault. It was almost as if he was out of his mind. I'd never seen him like that before.'

'Then what?'

'He got hold of me and...'

'Yeah?'

'He pushed my face down onto the lighted stove. And it burned away all my hair. Look.'

Louise pulled away her blonde hairpiece to reveal her bald scalp beneath. The skin had been replaced, but it was white with marks that continued right down onto her forehead. The cab driver stared into the mirror. Louise felt the car's wheels rumble along the edge of the grass verge.

'Guess why he was so angry,' she said.

'I don't know,' the cab driver said. 'I don't know why.'

'Just because, when he arrived at T-Man's house, stupid T-Man had changed his mind and wouldn't let him in. That was all!'

'He was disappointed then,' the taxi man said. 'But you're right. He did go too far. Not far for *us* now, though,' he added gratefully, 'we're nearly there.'

'But that wasn't the worst thing about that day.'

'I'm sure it wasn't, Ma'am. Are you sure you want to go on talking about it? You don't want to go working yourself up. That's not good.'

'Jeff must have been scared by what he'd done, because he just went away, out of the flat.'

'Just up this next rise and we're there.'

At the brow of the hill, Louise saw a massive white wall. The car slowed, they turned in through a gateway, and then she saw the house. It was white like the wall, but the shape of it was made up of curves and squares, like an art-deco house. It was surrounded by a forest of sick-looking trees.

'This is the place,' the taxi man said.

Louise leaned forward. 'Let me finish. You can leave your meter running. The thing was that I was sitting there with my head all burned, and I saw that the TV was showing Conway Johns' house, the place where Jeff had gone, and it was showing what had happened there later, after Jeff had come home. Conway Johns' house had been attacked by Morthwil, one of the Supervillains.'

'Yeah? I've heard of Morthwil. I remember hearing about him. Didn't know he was still alive.'

'The TV had all this video from the security cameras in Conway Johns' house, and it showed Morthwil in there. He came right through one of the walls, then he went and stood in the middle of each room, his arms sprang out like hammers, and he smashed and wrecked everything. He just went from room to room and smashed it all.'

'Yeah. I heard about that attack. But you should try and forget all that now.'

'And then Jeff came back into the kitchen. And I was sitting there with my head all black and bleeding, looking at Conway Johns' ruined house. I hoped Jeff was going to be sorry. I still hoped we could work things out, but Jeff just sat there and stared at the TV. He was fascinated.'

'Where is he now, this Jeff? I expect you're well away from him now?'

'That's right, he's back in Steel Ring City. He went away from me shortly after. It was less than a week after he went that I got the letter saying that this house was mine.'

The cab driver held the door for Louise and didn't look at her face while she put her wig back on. He carried her bags up to the front door and then quickly returned to his car.

Louise watched the car turn and drive away. She looked at the sick trees. Then she walked up the little path to the front door.

The door to Crystal House unlatched automatically and powered itself slowly aside. Louise picked up her bags and lifted them into a cool, quiet, circular hallway. She found she was still thinking about Jeff as she looked around. She swallowed, then breathed, and a calm feeling came to her all at once. Crystal House was like a fortress. She could stop running now. She could hide here and be safe from him.

Chapter Three

'Well hit, Sir!'

The cricket ball sailed across the sky. Robot AM-10 hurried to retrieve it, but the Young Master was in the lead now with 98 runs to the robots' 97.

U-3 bowled again. The Young Master swung his bat and once more hit the ball with a mighty crack. It flew straight towards U-3's arms only for the robot to miss the catch. The ball bounced away.

'Good shot, Sir!'

The Young Master made another run and now had 99.

U-3 bowled again, but this time the Young Master did not move. He just stood there, let the ball thud into the bat, and then stared at it rolling on the grass.

'Would you like to take another run, Sir?' AM-10 said.

The Young Master looked at him for a second before nodding and then running for the far wicket. Now the Young Master's score had reached a hundred, and so he'd won the game, as he always did, and it was time for tea.

The robots applauded the Young Master as he entered the banqueting hall. One of them presented him with a celebratory cake and a cricket trophy, but today the Young Master was beginning to feel that there might be something odd about all this. Perhaps he hadn't actually deserved to win after all. As AM-10 served his food, the Young Master looked up at the ceiling, with its bountiful mouldings of vegetables and fruit, and at the colourful tapestries around the walls, with their scenes of hunting from long ago. He looked at the rest of the robots sitting with him around the table, at their familiar faces and casings. He loved them all but, just for today, had the feeling that something was wrong.

'AM-10,' he suggested, 'may we play a cricket match again this evening?'

The attentive robot did not reply immediately. Pencil-drawing was what had been planned.

'More cricket, Sir?' the robot replied eventually. 'Very well.'

The evening game began with the Young Master opting to bowl, but he deliberately threw the ball away, far into the undergrowth.

'I'll get it!' he yelled as he ran into the trees while, behind him, the robots completed two runs. The Young Master found the ball and saw U-3 gesturing dumbly for him to throw it his way, but the boy ignored the robot and continued into the trees, brushing through the leaves and branches, feeling somehow as if they belonged to a world that was more real than his own. Then, ahead, he saw the Wall. He had forgotten that he would find the Wall here. But the Wall was important. Why was it important? He couldn't remember.

He returned to the game.

When the Young Master threw the next ball, AM-10 foolishly tapped it into his own stumps, so now it was the Young Master's turn to bat. The robots had done this before. The boy knew that now he would be batting for the rest of the game.

Then, as AM-10 gently bowled, the Young Master saw a gleaming shape in the trees. At first he thought it was one of the U- or AM-robots, but it was not. It shone too brightly. The ball crunched softly into the stumps. The Young Master realised he was seeing one of the silver women. What was that doing out here? Why had one of the silver women left the house? He had thought that they never moved.

'Perhaps we should discount that ball, Sir,' AM-10 said, but the Young Master also heard the faint clicking of robot conversation and saw the silver woman move obediently back towards the house.

'The interruption is over, Sir,' AM-10 said. 'Shall we now continue?'

'Oh, yes...' the Young Master replied vaguely, but he was tired of cricket now. He deliberately hit the next ball into the bushes again. U-3 found it immediately, but the Young Master ran the other way, towards the other side of the cricket lawn.

'That is not the way to run, Sir,' he heard AM-10's voice say behind him.

The boy ran across the daisy-covered grass. He remembered that he had copied some of those pretty flowers in a pencil drawing once. He pushed his way into dense greenery, through leaves, smelling the wood and the earth, feeling the sharp twigs scratching at his hands and face, until the Wall loomed up in front of him again.

U-5 appeared there, standing dumbly between the Young Master and the Wall, but, like all the U-robots, U-5 was slow, and the Young Master easily dodged past it. He slapped his hands onto the stonework and tried to climb, U-5's head clicking frantically behind him.

The Young Master turned and saw AM-10 running towards him. He tried to scramble up the Wall but was unable to get a proper footing and so dropped back to the ground. He stood by the Wall as AM-10 approached.

'Hello, AM-10. I thought I'd like a game of running and hiding,' the boy said. AM-10 bowed slightly. The Young Master began to feel foolish and smiled as the robot led the way back towards the cricket lawn.

'I've often wondered, AM-10,' the Young Master continued. 'What is it that lies beyond that wall?'

'Beyond the Wall? That is the End of the World, Sir.'

'Beyond this wall lies the Edge of the World? That sounds exciting!'

'No, Sir, I said that beyond the Wall is the *End* of the World. Come now, let us return to the game.'

Chapter Four

The alarm trilled musically as Louise left the shop, and she saw a security guard with a badge: 'My Name is JOE.'

'You, stop right there,' a thin triumphant smile crossed Joe's face. 'Let's see your bag.'

'I haven't taken anything.'

'Then you come up to the office and we'll check.'

Unable to believe what was happening, Louise was led through a side door. She had not stolen anything. She was on her first shopping expedition in Crescent City and had gone into a shop called 'Henry's Victual Store', where she hadn't found much that she'd wanted.

'OK. We'll check everything against your receipt, shall we?'

Louise could hardly believe the humiliation as she laid out her purchases for him to check against the receipt. It was a nightmare. She began to think that she might have accidentally stolen something. But then Joe finished pawing through her things and she started re-packing her bag.

'Your head,' he said. 'You're wearing a wig. What are you hiding under there?'

But then another door opened, and two men came out. One, a big-faced, fair-haired man in a powder-blue suit, spoke to the other.

'Still letting Joe out of his playpen, Henry? You'll end up in court one of these days if you keep letting him loose on your customers.'

For the first time, Joe looked sheepish.

'I didn't find nothing.'

'Good grief, Joe. Remember - only challenge if you see stuff actually being taken. Sorry, Ma'am. Yeah, Exeter, but my boys, they've got to start somewhere.'

The fair-haired man smiled at Louise.

'Welcome to Henry's Victual Store,' he said. 'I'm pleased to say I have nothing to do with the management here.'

He led Louise back downstairs.

'Poor old Henry,' he said when they got outside. 'He can't get anyone else to employ his sons, so he hires them himself as security guards.'

Louise looked at her rescuer.

'Who are you?'

'Exeter van Hoyland. I own the Peacock Motel down at the bottom of the hill.'

'I live on the top of the hill. I've just arrived from Steel Ring City.'

'You're not getting a very good welcome.' They reached a powder-blue car. 'Care for a ride back to the Peacock? And I'd be pleased to offer you dinner there by way of an apology from Crescent City. On the house.' He smiled again. 'On condition you don't really take poor old Henry to court.'

Louise laughed.

'Why were you there? In the shop?' she asked, just for something to say.

'I was getting Henry to sign up as a sponsor for this summer's Crescent City Superhero Festival.'

The Peacock Motel was wonderful. It would have looked futuristic a few years ago but now had a dated charm. Bubble lamps and fibre-optic lights flickered while big-framed windows gave a wide view of the lawns outside, where, sunning himself, there was a pure white peacock.

Exeter called a waitress and gave Louise a menu.

'I can't stay, but order anything you like,' he said, 'and remember, it's on the house.' He turned to go.

'Wait,' Louise said. 'Please stay if you would. I'd like someone to talk to.'

Exeter sat down opposite Louise. He recommended fish, and then ordered and poured some wine.

'So why have you come to live on our Superhero Hill?'

'I've come to a place called Crystal House. My aunt was Agnes Bale, who was the old 'Moon Queen', and she's just recently died.'

'The *Moon Queen*? She was the most beautiful woman in the world. I didn't know she'd died. I'm sorry about that.'

'It's alright. I never knew her. I still don't know much about her.'

'Well, if I can do anything to help you settle in, I'd be only too glad,' Exeter said. 'I'm honoured to meet the niece of such a famous neighbour.'

'Did you know her - my aunt? Crystal House is so close to your motel.'

'Afraid not. And I never even actually met her. No-one in Crescent City knew the people who lived up on the hill.'

Louise looked at the white peacock, now bobbing contentedly towards the window, then back at Exeter.

'So the rest of the houses up there are all like mine?' Louise asked. 'Fortresses, bunkers?'

'I don't think any of them originally planned to stay on in those houses when they grew old. They had the houses while they were all still active. It was just that when they retired, they never moved away.'

'Except Conway Johns,' said Louise, remembering Jeff's awful book. 'He never lived here. He always lived in Steel Ring City. That's where I come from.'

'Conway Johns,' Exeter said. 'The only one who could ever defeat Morthwil. And luckily all their battles took place in space or in the high stratosphere. If they'd fought on the earth there would have been tremendous destruction. I've seen videos of them fighting in the sky, like shadows in the clouds, and, from the ground, it sounded like thunder.'

Exeter went away and then, a few minutes later, returned with some brightly-coloured comics. On the cover of one was a beautiful woman wearing a purple cloak and a mask that covered the top half of her face. The comic was called 'Adventures of the Moon Queen'.

'This was her comic,' Exeter said, grinning. 'I've got nearly the whole run. I'm showing you this one because it shows the inside of Crystal House.'

Louise looked at the pictures. The high rooms in the house looked just as eerie as they did in real life.

'I've hardly found my way about,' she said. 'I had enough trouble at first just finding the light switches. It took ages to find some normal-looking rooms. In the upstairs part, where my aunt must have lived. In some ways, it is more like a fortress. It's hardly like a house at all. There's a massive chair all by itself in a big room right in the middle of the house. It looks like a giant padded coffin, standing upright.'

Exeter turned the pages of the comic, and Louise saw her beautiful aunt again, but now sitting in that hideous chair.

'The *Moon Chair*,' Exeter said.

'And there are some incredibly creepy statues,' Louise said. 'In the house, there are enormous statues of silver women.'

'I've never heard of them.'

Louise looked up at him. Then at the comic again.

'Is this true, what it says here about how my aunt and all the other Superheroes came to have powers in the first place?' she asked. 'I expect you'll know all about it.'

'Yes, they were all born at about the same time. All their parents had been on holiday in the Southern Mountains one summer, at a time of unusual solar flares. And when their children were born, they all turned out to have those fantastic abilities, and it's never happened again. T-Man got his strength, your aunt got her agility, the Die Master found that he could never be killed, the Golden Man and Glinda could swim for hours underwater, and nearly all of them could fly. But some of them became

Supervillains. Morthwil was the worst of that kind. Only T-Man could ever defeat him.'

'I don't want to hear about Morthwil,' Louise said. 'And at the moment, Exeter, I'm pleased that I live in a fortress.'

She found she was going to have to tell the tale of what Jeff had done to her again.

'I'm glad to hide away,' she said, 'because of what happened with my old boyfriend...'

Exeter listened gravely when she told him what Jeff had done. He listened as she told him about the TV and Morthwil attacking Conway Johns' house, and he didn't bat an eye when she removed the wig to reveal her scarred head, right in the middle of his busy restaurant.

Then they were sitting there in silence. All the other diners had stopped talking, only resuming when Exeter deliberately smiled around the room. Louise quickly put her wig back on.

'I must apologise,' Exeter said. 'I shouldn't have gone on about the Superheroes so much.'

'I apologise too. I didn't mean to upset your restaurant.'

'Don't worry about them. Most of them are regular customers. They won't mind.'

'This place is wonderful. Please tell me more about my aunt.'

'I'd like to do that. I have some things I keep here that I think may interest you.'

So after they had finished eating, Exeter led Louise through to the piano lounge, where, among the settees and palm plants, she saw the decorations on the walls - film posters, stills, and old newspaper stories, all of them about the Moon Queen.

'I call this the Moon Room,' Exeter said. 'Although I never met her...' His voice trailed off as he stood there amid his fabulous collection.

'Well, you did say that my aunt was the most beautiful of them all.'

Exeter led her to a corner by the very end of the bar, where a glass case stood. Inside was an unexpectedly heavy-looking costume, the costume of the Moon Queen.

'It wasn't hers,' Exeter said as he unlocked the case. 'It's from a film. Now, as a proper welcome gift,' he lifted the costume from its frame and placed it into Louise's arms, 'I'd like you to have it. A gift from Crescent City.'

Louise didn't reply. She was staring at the face mask, remembering how beautiful the Moon Queen had looked in the comic, and thinking of her own face.

After Exeter had ordered a taxi and Louise had gone back up the hill, agreeing to return to the Peacock soon, he stood by the window and looked at the sky with big white clouds coming over, towering into the blue. It was like a dream come true, the niece of the Moon Queen coming to his restaurant. He found himself hoping that his enthusiasm for Louise's aunt hadn't seemed too naive. But he wondered mostly about his gift. Had giving Louise that costume been the right thing to do? Was it an odd gift to give?

Chapter Five

The Young Master awoke early in the morning while the sun was still low, sending bronze light through the trees. He lay awake listening to the absolute silence of the house. The day had not yet begun. He got out of bed and dressed.

He peered out from his room into the empty corridor, then clicked the door silently behind him so that it looked as if he slept on. In the morning stillness, the boy felt for once that he was truly the *owner* of this house. He padded softly along the hallway towards the front door, looking up at the tapestries of hunting scenes and of people flying through the air. That looked so exciting. He had once asked AM-10 who those people were, but the robot had replied that he didn't know. Now the Young Master felt as if he half-remembered them. He wondered why, if he himself could almost remember those exciting people, the knowledgeable AM-10 could not.

He drew back the heavy bolts of the huge front door, then gently heaved it open.

U-3 was standing outside, inactive because it was so early. The Young Master went up to the familiar old robot, intending to tease him by waking him suddenly, but then he decided he would not. He would not speak and would make no sudden movement, because either of those things might stir U-3 into wakefulness, and then the day would have to begin.

The Young Master went to the cricket pitch and remembered how he had so easily won the game the day before. He saw some outbuildings, sheds he'd never been allowed to explore. He peered around cautiously, feeling guilty as he went up to the largest shed and tried the door. Of course, it was locked. Strange that he was the Young *Master,* but was not allowed into that place. There was an old wooden box nearby, and he dragged it beneath one of the windows. He stepped up onto the box and looked in.

He saw a long bench down the middle of the room. On it lay a familiar gleaming form, one of the enormous silver women, but this one was in two halves, parted at the waist. She looked vulnerable. The Young Master shivered with fearful excitement.

He jumped down from the box, fetched his cricket bat, and smashed the window. As he turned to throw the bat back down, he caught sight of U-3 in the distance, still standing still. The Young Master had been too worried for the silver woman to remember to be quiet, but fortunately U-3 seemed not to have noticed the sound.

Cautious to avoid the broken glass, the Young Master reached in the window, undid the latch, and climbed down. The table was almost too tall for him to see over. The boy lifted his hand to touch the silver woman and felt the metal. He had never actually wanted to touch one of the silver women before. He ran his fingers over the smooth surface and the sharp ridge where she had been parted in the middle.

Once outside again, the Young Master ran back towards the house, ready to begin the day and looking forward to telling AM-10 what he had found, but when he saw the top of the house, peeking over the trees, he thought that perhaps he'd better not tell AM-10 about this particular discovery after all. He turned away from the house.

The Wall was much too high to climb, so the Young Master followed it along until he saw another large shed. This one was of more decorative stonework, with buttresses, spires, and pinnacles, and it was built *through* the Wall. He could see where the roof continued on the other side, into the End of the World. Rows of stone statues were set into alcoves on each side of the elaborate porch. The door here was open.

Inside this building, it was like the Library, but without the books. The Young Master crept down the centre aisle towards where the rest of the building was blocked off by the Wall, and then, amazingly, he began to hear voices from the other side.

'*And we prayed,*' a voice said. '*We prayed that the world would not be consumed in a fury of fire and terror. That the peoples of the world would be spared, and we were granted that salvation by the Heroes.'*

The single voice was answered by many more.

'Amen.'

How marvellous this was! The Young Master could contain his excitement no longer.

'AM-10, AM-10!' he yelled shrilly as he ran out from that vast shed and back across the lawns. 'Guess what I've found!'

'It is not always a good idea to explore the grounds alone,' AM-10 said, 'and I regret that I had not previously instructed you that the chapel is strictly out of bounds.'

The Young Master looked puzzled.

'But I'm the Young *Master*, aren't I? Why should anywhere be out of bounds to me?'

'It is true that you are the Master,' AM-10 replied, 'but you are also *Young.'*

A gleaming shape moved towards them, one of the silver women. The silver woman spoke,

'It is time for the Young Master to awaken,' she said.

There was a long pause, and then AM-10 replied, 'No. It is not the time.'

'You are mistaken, AM-10. Events beyond the Wall have made his presence necessary. He must be awakened.' The silver woman went away, reflections from her body gleaming on the walls.

'What was all that about, AM-10?' the Young Master demanded. 'I'm already awake!'

Chapter Six

The whole road cracked and split as the Capital City bus came to a shuddering stop amid a cloud of burnt rubber from its tyres. The people piled off, screaming, as flames began to lick from underneath. Louise could hear sirens in the distance. Smoke poured from the nearby buildings, and she saw the entire frontage of one of them collapse into the street. The bus passengers ran towards the shops, still looking bewildered rather than properly scared, still thinking about their journeys and their errands. But then a burned-out car smashed down from the air into the pavement right by them, and they found the right degree of fear.

A blocky figure strode up the street, crushing the surface as it came.

'The Lead Coffin,' the newscaster said, while an unsuspecting cyclist sailed into the figure's path and was killed with a blow to the

head. 'The Return of the Lead Coffin caused carnage today on the streets of Capital City...'

Louise tried to force her eyes away from the TV, glad she was safe in Crystal House, but she could not keep from watching.

The Lead Coffin tore a news kiosk apart, and papers flew everywhere. He burst the sandstone cladding from the corner of another building. Bullets were raining into him, but he barely noticed them. His fist slammed into another skyscraper, making it shudder. Then a sticky burning substance poured onto him from a police weapon, setting his head on fire, but he did not pause in what he was doing.

A new view showed the Lead Coffin facing a group of news reporters. Then a closer picture showed his riveted grey body close up, the scorch marks and gouges on him almost enhancing his terrible invulnerability.

'*I return!* I return to challenge T-Man!' the Lead Coffin screamed. 'I return to challenge all the so-called 'Heroes' who remain. Come and stop me if you dare. My day resumes as yours ends!'

He raised his arms, screeched like a blunt drill through metal, and then lurched forwards.

The picture went black. Then the next view was from above, showing his trail of destruction, and then they were interviewing General Cranston, who said that, for now, he was observing protocol by keeping all his men well back.

Louise wondered why the army could not at least try to stop the Coffin. But then the TV showed a big armoured personnel carrier, and a closer shot showed the faces of all the soldiers inside, bloated and white and pressed up against the windows, a dark stain spreading across the road from beneath the vehicle.

The Lead Coffin roared again. He reared high above the camera, and then there was a view of him walking away from the city. Next, Conway Johns, *T-Man*, was being interviewed. His big handsome face had just finished saying something about the Lead Coffin. Then the interviewer asked him about Morthwil's attack on his own house that had happened in the weeks previously.

'I understood your house was well-defended?' the interviewer said.

'Yes,' Johns replied. 'I still have no idea how Morthwil penetrated my defences.'

'So your house was not as safe as legend has it?'

'I know nothing of legends,' T-Man smiled grimly. 'But nowhere in the world is truly impregnable, and neither are Lead Coffin or Morthwil invincible. They will be defeated.'

'I understand that you personally constructed all the defences of your own house, and the houses of your fellow Superheroes?'

'I built defences for my house and just one other - I built the defences of *Crystal House*, the residence of my colleague the Moon Queen.'

Louise gasped. The whole world seemed to pause. She could hardly believe what she had just heard, and she stared at the TV in horror, unable to wholly absorb what Conway Johns had just said.

'The Moon Queen, Agnes Bale, who recently died...' the TV interviewer continued, but Louise was no longer listening. She shut her eyes tight until she felt a roaring in her head. This was too much like before. She ran to the corner of the room and wedged herself between the wall and the floor.

'Don't hurt me!' she whispered, protecting her head as if it was again in flames. The only answering sound came from the TV, as they showed how the Lead Coffin had found the people who had escaped from the bus, trapped at the back of a shop. He had punched them, killing them instantly, one by one. They ought not to have shown that on TV. Louise felt moisture down her front and found that she had been sick.

Chapter Seven

'Happy Birthday, Sir!' AM-10 said as he strode into the Young Master's bedroom carrying a brightly wrapped parcel. Some of the other robots followed.

'Would you care to open your present now?' AM-10 said, handing it to him.

After unwrapping the present, which was a new train, AM-10 helped the Young Master dress, and then led him along the corridors, all decorated with streamers and flags, until they left the house by the front door.

'We will be holding your birthday breakfast on the lawn,' AM-10 said.

On long tables, plates were piled high with the Young Master's favourite foods. But, as AM-10 pulled out his chair, the boy looked up at the robot, puzzled.

'I thought my birthday was in the winter months?' he said. AM-10 paused in mid-motion, as if computing the best way to respond.

'Alas, Sir, the years go by so fast,' the robot said, but then his head began clicking.

'*AM-10 ---> AM-14, AM-12, AM-8, AM-3: Begin the entertainment.*'

The other AM- robots moved forward and stood in a line. Then they began to sing about the Young Master and his prowess at games, particularly cricket. The boy laughed in delight, not only because the song was about him, but because the beautiful music of the robots made him think of faraway places he had never seen. As the robot voices rose and fell, he envisioned distant cities and far-off seas. He smiled, almost crying with happiness. Truly, this was a wonderful day.

'I wish it could be my birthday every day, AM-10,' he said. Again, the robot did not reply immediately, as if again computing the most appropriate reply.

'It cannot be your birthday *every* day, Sir,' the robot said at last.

The food was served. During the meal, the Young Master listened as AM-10 explained about a new game he had invented called 'tennis'. He laughed at AM-10's inventiveness as the robot explained how the bats had stringed heads to allow them to move more quickly through the air. But then AM-10 turned away, even as the Young Master was still laughing, and all the robots fell silent. Among the distant trees, four of the silver women were approaching. Somehow the Young Master had an inkling of what was happening.

'They've come to spoil my birthday!' he shouted, 'Get rid of them!'

'AM-10 ---> Silver Control: Retire. This is not your place. Retire.'

But the silver women kept on coming. Several of them crossed the lawn to the long tables, moving swiftly and efficiently. They stopped right behind the Young Master's chair.

'It is time for the Young Master to awake. Deactivate yourself, AM-10. It is time for *Silver Control.*'

'I already *am* awake,' the Young Master yelled, 'Go away, you're spoiling my party!'

'AM-10 ---> Silver Control: Obey the direct command of the Young Master.'

But the silver women did not move.

'You must not distract the Young Master on his birthday,' AM-10 said. 'By remaining, you delay the games.'

'AM-10, AM-10,' the Young Master exclaimed. 'I've got an idea: *Tennis!* They could play. If we beat them, then they have to go!'

'Silver Control ---> AM-10: We have a fresh command from the Young Master.'

'We'll beat them, AM-10, and then they'll have to go away and leave us alone!'

The Young Master began his first-ever game of tennis against one of the silver women.

'All right, let's see what I do to *you*, you stupid thing,' he said. The boy hit the ball from the ground, using the racquet like a golf club. The ball made it over the net, but the silver woman sent it back effortlessly, and the Young Master missed it.

'Not fair, I wasn't ready!' he shouted. 'OK. You hit first this time.'

The silver woman served the ball gently, but the Young Master missed it again.

'That didn't count!' he shouted, unused to not winning easily. 'I can't reach that far. Come and help me, AM-10. Help me hit the ball back!'

AM-10 stepped onto the court, his head clicking.

'*AM-10 ---> Silver Control: Let the Young Master win the game.*'

'*Silver Control ---> AM-10: It is time for the Young Master to awake.*'

AM-10 hit the ball right over to the court, quicker than the silver woman could reach, and scored a point.

'A point to us!' the Young Master yelled jubilantly.

AM-10 managed to move the Young Master into the lead, but only by ignoring his angry shouts and completely taking over the game.

'Let me hit some, AM-10!'

The robot let the Young Master try for the ball again, but he missed it. The boy stamped off the court in a rage. Why had the silver woman started winning, and why wouldn't AM-10 let him play properly? He went and stood next to U-3 with tears in his eyes.

'I hate those stupid silver women. They're spoiling everything.'

AM-10 pushed the score ahead but then began to drop behind. The Young Master was horrified. His eyes flicked from AM-10 to the silver woman, then back again. Then he seemed to think of something, and a broad smile crossed his face.

'I'm on the silver women's side now. I want to be on the side that wins!' He ran back onto the court and stood there next to her.

The silver woman hit the ball again, and AM-10 missed it completely.

The Young Master looked up at the silver woman.

'We're winning,' he said. 'First side to a hundred points wins!'

AM-10 lost every ball after that, and the silver woman soon gained the hundred.

'We win! We win!' the Young Master cheered joyfully. 'You stupid AM-10, we've won!'

He looked up at the silver woman and then back to where AM-10 stood, defeated, on the other side of the net, and suddenly felt sorry.

'No, wait,' he called. 'It's a draw. Everyone wins. That's best. That's fair!'

'Silver Control ---> AM-10: Honour the terms of the game set by the Young Master. We will now take him for awakening.'

'AM-10 ---> Silver Control: I forbid it.'

The other three silver women stepped forward.

'AM-10 ---> All AM-series and U-series: Code Red: Prepare to defend the Young Master.'

As one, the house robots turned abruptly to face the silver women. The Young Master wondered what was happening now.

'It was only a game,' he said.

The two groups of robots faced each other in silence until, eventually, the four silver women turned away. The Young Master was glad that things seemed to be returning to normal, but then he saw an amazing sight. A gleaming of more metal among the trees. There were many, many more of the silver women watching from over there.

Chapter Eight

Louise pushed open the door of the Peacock Motel, shivering despite the heat of the sun. She ran up to the desk without gaining any comfort from the decorations, the colours, or the plants.

'Is Exeter here?' she asked, but her voice cracked into a sob. The girl at the desk looked at her in surprise.

After babbling that it was her turn to buy lunch and dragging Exeter into his own restaurant, not even thinking that he might have been busy, Louise stared at him across the table. He smiled back and prepared to listen.

'Did you see all that stuff about the Lead Coffin on TV yesterday?' Louise said. 'He completely destroyed part of Capital City. And then T-Man... Conway Johns, came on and...'

'...and he mentioned Crystal House.' Exeter smiled reassuringly. 'Yes I saw that part, but I don't think it meant anything. The Lead

Coffin mainly just damaged buildings. Most people got away in plenty of time, and then he vanished.'

'But what about those soldiers and the people in that shop being killed? And he's not gone forever. I'm really frightened!'

'The Lead Coffin is terrible,' Exeter said, 'but I'm sure it's just a coincidence that T-Man mentioned Crystal House. In any case, if your house has defences built by T-Man himself, you should feel very safe.'

'Morthwil got into T-Man's house.'

'Yes, but even so I'm sure you're quite safe. Crystal House must be one of the most secure places in the world.'

A loud argument had begun at a nearby table. Louise saw the security guard, Joe, who had arrested her in Henry's Victual store. He was with a younger boy, and they were arguing with one of the waitresses. Exeter watched, but the waitress was coping with them.

'You'll recognise Joe,' Exeter said. 'The other one is his little brother, Carl.

'Crescent City is a lovely town,' Exeter continued, 'and, as I told you, we hold a

Summer Festival every year, so that's coming up soon.'

Louise gradually forgot her fears as Exeter talked about running the motel and about the Summer Festival, which was all about the Superheroes. Exeter was modest, but Louise understood that he himself did most of the organisational work. Perhaps that was because he was so approachable. People found it easy to trespass on his time, as she was doing now.

That reminded her of the gift he'd given her, the costume of the Moon Queen. She was about to speak, to thank him for it again, but Exeter stood up. Joe and Carl had started making remarks about one of the other diners. Louise watched as Exeter politely escorted them out of the room, but it was none of her business so she looked away.

Today the white peacock was not in sight. Louise looked for it and then focused on the edge of the trees. These were the same trees that led back up the hill to Crystal House. She craned her neck round to look at more trees. They looked so much more healthy and lush down here than at Crystal House. Exeter returned.

'All sorted out. They thought they could come here and behave how they like because their father's helping sponsor the Summer Festival.'

An elderly woman appeared, dressed in blue.

'Hello, Exeter,' she said. 'Who's your friend?'

'Mrs. Briggs, meet our new neighbour, Louise Bale, niece of the famous Moon Queen. She's come to live on the hill at Crystal House. Louise, this is Mrs. Briggs, one of my most valued customers.'

Mrs. Briggs said hello and then went away.

'Did you have to tell her that, Exeter?' Louise said. 'I know Crystal House is probably super-safe, but I'm still scared. I'm scared of the house and of those awful silver statues, and I'm not sure I want people to know where I live yet, or know who I am.'

Exeter opened his mouth to apologise, but Louise carried on.

'This morning,' she continued, 'someone came to the front door. The bell rang, but when I went to answer it, there was no one there. I went right outside and looked around. I even went around the garden a bit and into the trees. And those trees are all half-dead, with creepers and moss growing all over them, not like the ones down here. I thought children might be playing or something. I called out, but no one answered. So then I went down to the gateway to see if anyone was there, and I saw a car, just parked by the side of the road.

'There was someone in it, but he had all the windows closed and it was difficult to see inside, and there were lots of flies out there, all buzzing around my face. I went right up to the car, and whoever was in there just let the window down a tiny bit. He kind of whispered to me that he'd broken down, but then he started the engine and drove away. And those flies kept coming, kept landing on my hands and on my face.'

Exeter looked as if he didn't quite know what to say.

'It sounds odd,' he said, 'but perhaps he *was* just someone who had broken down?'

'No. It wasn't a normal person. Because how did he suddenly get his engine going? When I first saw the car, the engine was switched right off, and he started it up when he saw me. It was as if he knocked on the front door of Crystal House and then went away and hid in his car, as if he just wanted to bring me out of the house, just to have a look at me.'

Exeter looked doubtful, almost as if he was wondering whether Louise was making it all up, and when they reached the dessert, he was called away again.

While she waited for Exeter to return, Louise looked around and saw a TV out by the reception desk. It was showing the Lead Coffin's attack on Capital City again. She saw T-Man's face, speaking about the attack. They were replaying the interview where he had mentioned Crystal House. Then the TV showed President Rayonier and pictures from the war in the Oil Lands to the south, and then the Supervillains again, as if it was all part of the same story.

A gleam of white caught her eye. The peacock bobbed up close to the window and looked at her in a friendly, dopey way. She was still looking at it when Exeter returned.

'I love your peacock, Exeter.'

'Well, please come here any time you'd like to see him, and it'll be my turn to get lunch next time.'

'I will come again,' Louise replied. She admired not only the peacock, but also Exeter's charm, and his professional skill as the owner of this curious little motel.

Chapter Nine

In the playroom, the Young Master switched the points and sent his new blue train flying onto the high-level route. He whooped with delight as it completed its triumphant circuit over the bridges while AM-10's green train had to stop and wait. He and AM-10 had been racing the trains all afternoon.

'Congratulations, Sir,' AM-10 said, but then the familiar clicking began in his head.

'U-3 ---> AM-10: Silver Control not responding. Four on their way to you.'

AM-10 clicked an acknowledgment and then spoke aloud to the Young Master.

'A little cool, is it not, Sir?' he said. 'Perhaps we should close the door and windows?'

'I'll do it.' The Young Master went to push the door shut, and the lock clicked automatically. But then, as he closed the window, he hesitated, admiring the view outside.

'I may win on the next timetable, Sir,' AM-10 warned, making the Young Master rush back to his controls.

The trains stood ready for the starting signal again, and then someone knocked at the door. But the signals went green. AM-10's green train powered ahead and reached the curve first. The Young Master yelled in annoyance. The tapping at the door came again, louder this time, but neither of them paid it any attention. The Young Master's train was now so close to AM-10's that he had to concentrate hard on his driving so as not to derail on the curves. The tapping resumed, a dull booming this time.

'Bother them!' the Young Master cried, 'Why can't they go away and leave us alone?'

With a crash, AM-10's train left the rails.

'A disaster for the green train, Sir,' the robot said and then continued, 'I do believe that in our excitement we have let ourselves become late for Tea. Let us use the secret passage to the kitchens.'

A hidden panel in the wainscoting slid back, and AM-10 ushered the Young Master quickly to the hole as the beating on the playroom door grew even louder. The panel clipped shut behind them, and, in the narrow passageway beyond, a row of lights came on.

When they reached the kitchens, AM-10 suggested that it was such a beautiful afternoon that Tea should be served in one of the old fortress rooms high in the roof, where there would be a fine view. This surprised the Young Master as AM-10 usually discouraged visits to the upper reaches of the house. When they got up there, it turned out that the robot had overestimated what they would be able to see from the white-painted room. The Young Master could hardly even reach the narrow windows at all. AM-10 unfolded a small table and chair and set out the Young Master's food, but then his head clicked continuously throughout the meal. The Young Master looked at him in annoyance, unaccustomed to being ignored. The clicking had completely taken over.

'AM-10, you are dull.'

There was a muffled rumbling and a vibration that shuddered through the floor.

'What's happening?'

AM-10 replied for the first time in several minutes, 'Nothing, Sir. Just some cleaning in progress in the rooms below.'

But now the whole room was shaking. There was a loud crash at the door. It burst open. Four of the silver women entered the white cell and towered over AM-10.

'It is time,' one of them said.

The Young Master looked up at them in awe, then at AM-10, who stood up.

'AM-10 ---> Silver Control: It is I who will decide when it is time to awaken the Young Master. AM-10 ---> All AM-series and U-series robots: Code Red: Request Assistance.'

Moving very quickly, one of the silver women stepped quickly past AM-10 and gently lifted the Young Master from his seat. Then she carried him off towards the door. The Young Master scrabbled for a grip on her smooth silver surface, trying to get free. He could hear AM-10 commanding the women to release him, but suddenly he found this exciting! This was *really* exciting! His eyes flashed eagerly as the women bore him down the corridors, pushing AM- and U-robots out of their way. The Young Master laughed in delight. The silver women left the house and sped across the lawns. The air outside held all the promise and excitement of summer, the colours of the flowers seemed extra bright, and the blue sky arched overhead. If the Young Master's new birthday year was going to be all like this, he was going to have a wonderful time. But there was one important thing he did not yet know.

'How old am I?' he asked.

But the silver women were running too quickly to speak. They rushed across the grass. The Young Master saw a big crowd of them ahead. Then there was a muffled thump from back by the house, the sound of something flying through the air, then a burst of flame and smoke came from amid the silver crowd, and several of them fell down. The Young Master's eyes were wide with wonder. This was all completely new. The women carrying him turned aside and made for the cover of some trees. Then they stopped there, perfectly still, as the rest of the women began to surge towards the house. The Young Master watched as the lines of silver women and house robots met, but then there was a horrible cracking sound and more smoke. He felt completely confused about all this, wondering what to do now.

He cheered.

'Go back over there! Go back! I want to see,' he shouted. He felt a tremor run through the silver woman who was carrying him, as if she wanted to obey but was being constrained by a stronger command.

'Take me back there!' he repeated. He felt another mechanical shiver pass through the woman. Some of the others began to obey, but their movements were slow.

'Hurry up, I don't want to miss anything!'

Smoke rose from the battle lines. The silver women were forcing the house robots back.

'Take me back there!'

The woman carrying him began to move back towards the house. The battle was nearly over. But then the Young Master saw a terrible sight. The familiar shape of AM-10 lay broken on the ground.

'AM-10!' he yelled. The silver woman set him down. All at once the remaining conflict ceased. All the robots and all the silver women came to a stop.

The Young Master knelt and touched AM-10's broken frame.

'AM-10?' he whispered. But there was nothing to be done. AM-10's head and frame were smashed, and his personality circuits were clearly visible inside. As his familiar world dissolved, the Young Master felt the silver women lift him up again and carry him away. Through his tears, he saw that they were carrying him towards the outbuildings where he had seen a silver woman who had been separated into two halves.

'Don't cut me in half!' he yelled, but then one of the women was whispering to him. She told him that they would do the opposite. She told him that he was incomplete, and that they were going to make him whole again.

Chapter Ten

'I knew you wouldn't believe me,' Louise laughed as she looked into Exeter's face.

'He could have been just what he said he was. He could have been just a baker,' Exeter said as the waitress brought their food.

'When you're standing at the front door of Crystal House in the morning, you just can't see the face of anyone who's standing there,' Louise said. 'The sun's right behind them. At first, I just thought he was shy. He was telling me about how he was new and was trying to establish his business and did I want to order any bread. I said no, but then he went on about how it was his first day, so then I said yes, just to get rid of him. Looking back, I can see what he was doing. It wasn't taking him long to wear me down.

'Then he got this square little notepad out. I kept looking at it. There was no other writing in there, as if Crystal House was the first place he'd ever called.

'So what did you do then?'

'I asked him his name and where he came from, in case he had an identity card or anything, and he told me an address that I can't remember. But the creepiest thing was that he gave me a funny little smile when he said it, as if he was pleased he'd been able to come up with an answer so quickly.'

'Well, there's one way of telling if he's genuine - if he does bring you some bread.'

'I didn't order any in the end. He asked me my name, but then his pencil broke when he started to write it down. But it was as if he'd deliberately pressed too hard and broken it. He kept apologising, and I found I was agreeing to go back into the house and get him something to write with. He had me so that I didn't know what I was doing. He was hypnotising me with that clean little book, waving it about in front of my eyes. But luckily I had enough sense left to keep watching him, and I saw him sort of *lean* forward. He didn't move his feet, but it was like he was about to follow me inside, so I turned around and... I shouted at him to go away.

'But he looked so hurt. I hadn't expected to feel sorry for him. It was just that he'd pushed me too far. So then I was about to say yes, come in after all, when I realised he's done it *all* deliberately. He'd deliberately annoyed me so that I'd get angry and then I'd feel sorry so that I'd overreact and end up doing just what he wanted. So I just closed the door shut in his face. I was beaten down, Exeter. I stood on the inside of that door, shaking, for ages. What do you think? Was it really someone trying to get into Crystal House, or am I going mad?'

Chapter Eleven

The silver women opened the door and carried the Young Master into the outbuilding. He remembered the two halves of a silver woman he had once seen on the table in here, but now the room was brightly lit, and she was gone, as if she had been made whole again. *As was going to happen to him*, the Young Master thought, although he did not understand how the women were going to make that happen. A sound and a pulse of pumping of machinery began, and then there was a massive clicking of robot conversation among the women. The Young Master wished he could understand what was being said. The clicking grew more rapid, more angry. He was tired now. He wasn't interested in being made whole, he just wanted everything back the way it was meant to be.

Then a sparking crack echoed around the place, the sound of pumping stopped, and all the silver women turned around as one. Had they changed their minds? The Young Master felt lost as the gleaming legs of the women swept around him like a forest of silver trees. Then he saw robot U-5 standing there by some equipment that stood near the table. Part of the equipment was smoking, as if the robot had damaged it. U-5 had stopped the silver women from making him whole.

The silver women closed in on U-5, smashed him to the floor, and broke off his head. They lifted up the Young Master and carried him back out of the shed and out through the grounds again. The house appeared ahead, but now it looked subtly different - the windows were all shuttered. Some remaining house robots stood around, burnt and damaged, but a faint crackle of electricity still hung between them. The silver women stopped some distance away and began their clicking again. The Young Master could tell by the repetition of the pattern that they were trying to speak to the house robots but were receiving no reply. The clicking continued for a while, but then stopped. The women had given up.

Then they began to move again. They carried the Young Master away from the house, moving deep into the woods. The sun still beamed complacently overhead, casting flickering and bewildering shadows. The Young Master cried out, but the four women who were carrying him still paid no attention.

When they came to the Wall, the women scaled it effortlessly, easily handling the Young Master across. Going over the Wall was what the boy had wanted to do for as long as he could remember, but now that it was happening it felt like nothing. On the other side of the Wall, the silver women ran with him again, but soon the trees opened out, and they came to a stop. A broad, smooth path with a broken white line down the middle stretched across in front of them, vanishing among the trees to either side. There came a roaring sound, and the silver women stepped quietly behind the boles of the trees to wait while a car went by. They crossed when the road was completely clear. Then, after more trees, they found another wall. Again they easily crossed the obstacle, but beyond this second wall the trees were denser, uglier, older, and more untidy. The undergrowth had run wild, as if this was a place where no one ever came. The Young Master remembered his games, thinking what a super place this would be to play, to hide. The trees were bluey-coloured and sick-looking. The silver women were careful with the Young Master and kept the sharp whipping branches safely away from him.

'Where are we going?' he asked, although by now he expected no reply.

Then they stopped, as if the Young Master's voice had changed everything, and he saw that a real woman was standing there ahead of them among the undergrowth. She was not silver. She was made of flesh and she wore a purple mask and a long cape.

Chapter Twelve

Louise saw Exeter at the reception desk.

'Thank goodness you've arrived,' he said. 'My stomach's been telling me it's time for lunch.'

They went through to the restaurant, and Louise saw that their usual table now had a small sign on it saying 'Reserved'.

'The season's getting busier,' Exeter explained when he sat down, 'but that's good, and the weather's holding up well.'

Exeter was ready to hear if she had another strange story to tell. She looked into his face, watching for any change in his expression when she told him she had.

'It was a milkman this time.'

'What did this milkman do?'

'He asked if I wanted any milk. He looked more normal than the bread man, but I was especially suspicious, so I just said 'no', and then he asked me if he could leave his card in case I changed my mind. I thought that, if his card gave a proper address, it would prove he was a real milkman, so I was beginning to think he might be OK. And when he put his hand into his pocket to get the card, I thought I would order some milk after all, because it would be good to at least have one person, one normal person, regularly call. So I said I'd like one carton every day, but then I noticed that he had no van or anything. He was just there, alone.

'What did it say on his card?'

'He never gave it to me. That's the thing. As soon as he reached into his pocket he must have seen in my face that his bluff had worked.'

'His bluff? Why do you think people are trying to get into Crystal House?'

'I don't know. You do believe me, don't you?'

Outside the window, the peacock was there. It slowly fanned its feathers into a magnificent display. All around the restaurant, people stopped eating to look at it, to remark on its beauty, but Exeter kept facing Louise as if to prove he would not be distracted from what she was saying.

'I want to hear anything you've got to say, Louise. And I'll believe whatever I want to believe. So tell me what happened next.'

'Well, he never got that card out, but I said OK, one carton per day, and then he asked me what my full name was and what was the full address of Crystal House. I told him, and then he wrote it down, and then he went away. The pad he was writing on, though, was just like the baker's.'

Louise saw the shape of Mrs. Briggs loom up behind Exeter. The older woman smiled benignly and made a shape with her mouth as if to say *love birds!* before she saw the peacock and got interested in that.

'From what you've told me it doesn't sound suspicious at all,' Exeter said.

'That's right, not suspicious at all. Apart from him being a milkman and not having a van, and having another of those creepy little writing-pads.'

'Perhaps he did have a van. Perhaps he left it out on the road. Perhaps he thought it would look presumptuous if he drove it up to your house the first time when he was soliciting for an order. Wait until tomorrow before you decide. If you get your milk, I'd say he was genuine.'

'He never gave me that card though. I'm sure he didn't have one. And what if there really *is* something wrong with him, but he gets me some milk anyway? It's not such a big deal to get someone some milk. One carton. If someone's tried two different disguises already - three if he was the man in the car - what's so hard about buying a carton of milk to bring it to me?'

Chapter Thirteen

'Why are you here? Why do you enter the grounds of Crystal House?' The beautiful woman in the mask stood in front of the silver women and the Young Master. The silver women carrying the boy trembled, as if ready to surge forward.

'Please command them to stay still,' the masked woman said.

The Young Master whispered shyly to the silver women to be still, and, to his surprise, felt the tension in them vanish.

'Why have you come this way, Theo? Are you re-formed and reawakened?'

'I'm not asleep,' he said. 'And why are you calling me 'Theo?' I'm the Young Master.'

'There's something wrong with this, Theo. This isn't how it's meant to be. You shouldn't be wandering away from your house still believing you're a child.'

'What do you mean?'

'Your Silver Control robots have obviously failed to restore your memory. Your real name is Theo Banks, and you were also known as the *Die Master*. You were given that name because you're always physically young and can never be killed.'

He stared at the beautiful woman in bewilderment. He felt he was in love with her, but why did she have to make things so complicated?

'It's not my fault,' he said. 'I was brought. Who are you, anyway?'

'My name is Agnes Bale. I am the Moon Queen. Now let us return to your house to see why you have emerged unrestored. Please command Silver Control to return you to your fortress.

'They brought me,' the Young Master said. 'They killed AM-10. He and the others are just... empty now, I think, back by the house.'

'Tell Silver Control to obey you, Theo. They belong to you.'

'Do as I say,' whispered the Young Master to the woman who was carrying him, and he found that it was true. She bowed her head.

Then the Moon Queen led the boy and his robot women back home.

'Instruct Silver Control to wait here,' the Moon Queen said, and then she went to the edge of the trees to look across the lawns at the Young Master's house. The remaining house robots still stood near the door, with a faint buzz of electricity between them. The Young Master followed the Moon Queen for a few steps because, for a moment, with her authority, this woman reminded him of AM-10. She knew exactly what to do. He reached up to try and hold her hand, but she then whirled around and slapped him away.

'Don't touch me, Theo,' she snapped. 'Never try that again!'

Bewildered, the Young Master watched as the Moon Queen walked slowly across the grass towards the house. She stopped several times, as if listening and checking that the sound of the house robots' electrical buzzing had not changed.

The Young Master stared at his old home, where the doors and windows were now shuttered and blind. He looked at the place where AM-10 had fallen, but the robot's casing had been taken away. He wanted to run out, to follow the Moon Queen and tell her to hurry up and make everything alright again, but he held back.

The Moon Queen was almost at the front door, but now the house robots' heads all slowly swivelled to follow her progress as she crept right up to the wall beside it.

Then the buzzing changed. An electric crack filled the air, and the Moon Queen was blasted back, away from the door. The Young Master shut his eyes in shock. One of the silver women sprang to life and sprinted across the grass. She ran straight to the Moon Queen, picked her up, and returned with her to the shelter of the trees. The Moon Queen's shoulder was blasted and burned. As the silver woman set her down, she began cursing, took a tiny container from a pocket in her cape, and started to apply a salve from it to her wounds.

'What happened?' the Young Master asked.

'Shut up,' the Moon Queen said. 'Tell one of *those* to obey only me.'

'Do as she says,' the Young Master told one of the silver women.

'Come,' the Moon Queen commanded, and the silver woman followed her back across the lawn.

The Moon Queen's walk across the grass looked very open and exposed this time. She paused just beyond the striking range of the house robots and told the silver woman to move away to one side. The Young Master watched, fascinated, as the house robots' heads turned to follow the silver woman, who was making graceful rings with her arms like a dancer, while the Moon Queen padded cautiously the other way.

Then the house robots began to almost imperceptibly move towards the silver woman, to slowly bring her within range. She did not back away. The Young Master opened his mouth to shout out a warning, but a silver hand covered his face. The silver woman who whirled her arms did not move away.

The Moon Queen darted forward with incredible speed. She reached the house door and rammed a small device from her cape into the lock, and the door opened wide. The house robots finally sensed what was happening, but they were too slow, their main attention still on the dancing silver woman. Their buzzing grew louder, but now the Moon Queen was inside the house.

The Young Master tried to run forward, but the silver women next to him still held him fast. Then the buzzing of the house robots faded away. The Moon Queen appeared back in the doorway.

'You can come here now, Theo,' she called, and then ungratefully snapped her fingers under the nose of the silver woman who had danced.

The Moon Queen had switched off all the house robots with some control system in the house. She shoved the Young Master ahead of her.

'Your real name is Theo Banks,' she told him again, 'and you are a Superhero called the Die Master who can never be killed. You live here in this big house, and your house robots have to keep wiping your mind to keep you sane in your child's body.

'But in times of crisis, the Silver Control robots are meant to awaken you. But you've never been anything but trouble. I knew this juvenile-life idea of yours would all go wrong. I wish you had stayed in the asylum.'

The Moon Queen popped open a panel in one of the walls and flicked some switches. Then she went from room to room, the Young Master following her, until she found a deactivated robot, AM-12. She flipped open a panel on its head and examined the circuits inside.

'One of your favourite robots remains fully intact, Theo,' she said, 'and that's U-3.' She pressed a red button inside AM-12's head. 'Let's bring him to us.'

The Young Master said nothing until, minutes later, U-3 came into the room. He stopped in front of them and switched himself off.

The Moon Queen removed her hand from the circuits inside AM-12's head and then opened a similar panel on U-3. She pulled out a rack of circuits and changed some tiny switches. Then she took the Young Master back to the room with the wall panel, where she clicked back the switches the other way.

'Now U-3 will repair the rest of your robots as best it can,' she said.

'Will he be able to repair AM-10?' the Young Master asked hopefully.

'AM-10, the mentor robot,' she said. 'Let's go and find him.'

She led the Young Master from the house in the direction of the outbuildings.

There was nothing new to see, just the table and the disabled machinery and the remains of robot U-5 on the floor. But then the Moon Queen opened a small door at the back of the outbuilding. There was a small yard outside there surrounded by a high fence, and all around the yard there were robot parts. The Moon Queen went to look at some of them and then picked up a robot head.

'This is what's left of AM-10,' she said, 'and it's impossible to revive him.'

Chapter Fourteen

'Louise, has anyone else called?' said Exeter van Hoyland as she came towards the restaurant. She lifted her head up to him and, to his dismay, he saw that she looked terrified.

'This time it was a little girl,' Louise said, as Exeter guided her to their table, his hand on her arm. 'I was waiting to see if I was going to get any milk, like you said. I'd already checked outside once, but there was nothing there.

'And then the bell rang. I was ready for anything. I'd decided to wait a long while before I opened the door, long enough for anyone normal to go away. But I heard crying, so I had to look, and it was a little girl out there.'

'Did you get your milk?'

'No. There was no milk. There hasn't been any milk at all, and you know I didn't expect there to be. But this little girl was there, just crying her eyes out and saying that her father's car had just crashed on the road and she thought he was dead. She said he'd gone through the windscreen and she needed to use the phone. She tried to run past me and get into the house.'

'Was her father OK?'

'It wasn't real, Exeter. At first, I was going to let her in because she looked so scared, but then I thought back to the other callers, and so I wanted to ask her something to make her prove that she was real, but I couldn't think of anything while she was standing there screaming at me. So I started telling her, 'OK, I'll let you in, but only because it's an emergency.' I was trying to sort it out in my head, but then that little girl tried to push me back out of her way. And that's what brought me to my senses. I shut the door on her, but she kept screaming at me from outside about all the blood and about seeing her father's brain in his broken skull. And then she went quiet and I stood there for ages. I thought, what if she was real? Was her father going to die because of me? I wanted to go out and find her and tell her to try at one of the other houses.

'But listen, Exeter. Then I thought back, and I realised that there had been something so wrong. She'd looked just like a little girl, except that she was much too *big*. I didn't notice at first because I was looking down at her from the step. But she was the size of a small adult. And then I remembered that her hands had been tiny, and the hands of the other callers had been tiny too.'

Exeter smiled gently.

'Would you like to take one of the rooms here at the Peacock tonight, free of charge?'

Louise looked at him as if she didn't know how to take that. He was very generous, but had he believed what she'd said?

'That's very nice of you, Exeter, but no thanks. If I did come here I'd pay you, but I'm not leaving Crystal House empty while those strangers are calling.'

'Then I have another suggestion, Louise. Why don't I call round myself at Crystal House tomorrow, early, and wait with you to see if anyone else comes to the door?'

When Louise left the motel, the sun was shining, and the day looked innocent, so she decided to walk home. She followed the road back up the hill, but the sound of the passing cars disturbed her. She felt vulnerable by the carriageway. The cars kept swishing by, and she remembered the fake little girl screaming about the crash.

To take her mind off the road, she began looking at the trees, watching how they got visibly sicker-looking as she ascended the hill. The boles were twisted into weird shapes and had swellings and unexpected soft parts, as if a cancer had infected them. Louise began to actively hate the cars and the trees. She saw the trees here as a disgusting growth on the face of the world. And then she thought that soon she would change the grounds of Crystal House. She would destroy all those trees.

She tried to imagine what Exeter would say if she told him she was going to do that. And then she began wondering why he was always so friendly to her. What did he want? Why was he being such a good friend? He had not told her the exact time he would be calling in the morning. And then she remembered that she had never looked at the size of his hands.

Chapter Fifteen

Some weeks after she had first met the Young Master, the Moon Queen led all the silver women across the lawns, away from the Young Master's house. As the silver robots walked, the setting sun gleamed redly on their casings, and the Young Master watched wistfully until the last of them was gone from sight. His remaining house robots were now nearly all repaired, and they alone would look after him now. Except for AM-10. He was unrepairable.

A bird's call echoed in the trees. Squirrels came out and played on the lawns.

He went to the room where his train set was kept, pulled open the cupboard, and looked at all the trains, the rails, and the bridges, stacked tidily in their boxes. He had no idea how to assemble the railway, because AM-10 had always done that.

In the failing light, he went outside again and looked at all the places where he had played games. AM-10 had always had new ideas for them. He longed for AM-10 to be alive again, but then he had a different idea. He remembered some of the things AM-10 had always forbidden. Perhaps he could now explore some more of the upper storeys of the house, or take another look at the Library, from where, ever since he had discovered it, AM-10 had firmly kept him away.

He stood in the hallway and looked at all the hangings on the walls, the tapestries of the hunting scenes. He saw the people and the hills. Then he began to look for the images of people flying through the air.

He found one, a man in a mask. He decided to count them to see how many he could find. Along the main corridor, he found five flying people in all. Then he touched the banister and looked up at the faraway ceiling, high above the stairwell, right at the top of the house. A big faded sun was painted up there. He began to climb. He saw no more images of flying people for a while until, on the third floor, he found two more on tapestries on either side of a window. That made seven. He looked out of that window and saw the lawns and trees, glowing amber in the setting sun.

Higher up, the house was silent. All the little sounds of his robots quietly moving about had been replaced by just the feel of the slow movement of air. He went on up until he reached the top, where the staircase ended. Here was just a railing and the big painted sun close above his head. It was darker up here, despite the painted sun. The windows here were shuttered.

The Moon Queen had insisted that his real name was Theo Banks, that he was the 'Die Master', and that he could never be killed. Heights could not hurt him. He wondered why AM-10 had discouraged him from coming this high in the house. He wondered if he dared try and open the shutters.

AM-10 was gone. The Young Master pulled back the slats and then leaned out. There was no glass, just an opening to the sky. But then there was a new and exciting mystery. Down there, miles away, was a vast expanse of water, and along the curve of it were thousands of specks of coloured light.

At supper, the Young Master spoke to U-3. The U-robot could not reply, but he had been the Young Master's favourite after AM-10. He began to tell U-3 about what he had done, about how he had counted the tapestries with flying people and then gone up the stairs, and of the water and the lights he had seen. As he spoke, he began to think that U-3 was almost easier to speak to than AM-10 had been, because U-3 did not keep trying to guide his thoughts away from what he wanted to talk about. U-3 just listened, although his head began clicking. That slightly annoyed the Young Master, so he told U-3 what the Moon Queen had said, that his real name was Theo Banks and that he had once been known as the Die Master.

After supper, the Young Master led U-3 through the house, pointing out some of the flying people. His confidence growing, he opened an ever-locked door. Then his voice faltered and his words trailed off. It was another tapestry of a flying person, and he recognised it - far more elegant than the rest of them. It was the Moon Queen. He craned upwards to peer at the tapestry until his face was so close that the image vanished and he saw only coloured threads.

He opened his mouth to speak to U-3 but then saw that many more house robots had appeared nearby. He grinned. This picture of the Moon Queen must be really important for *all* the robots to come and see him. AM-12 stepped forward.

'Sir?' the robot enquired. The Young Master saw that AM-12 had extended his arm as if he wanted to take him away.

'What are you doing, AM-12?'

But now the robot gripped his hand and pulled sharply, and the Young Master was being led towards the front door.

'Is this a new game, AM-12?'

The front door opened for them, and the Young Master was led out into the darkness. He looked up at the stars. He thought again of the Moon Queen. And then he seemed to remember flying among the stars himself, like on the tapestries, up there with those other flying people. Once, he remembered, he had lived in the sky. He wanted to tell AM-12 about that, but then he stopped. He saw where the house robots were taking him. They were approaching the outbuildings again. He remembered the half-woman, U-5 damaging the machinery, and then the robot battle and the remains of beloved AM-10 that were now lying in the yard behind.

'Let go of me!' he said. 'I'm the Young Master, and you have to do as I say!'

The robots opened the door and forced him inside. He felt terror at what the robots were going to do. He saw the table ahead surrounded by its repaired equipment. U-3 was already there. The pumping sound that he had heard before began again.

'Are you going to make me whole? Like the silver women were going to? What's happening, U-3?' he demanded, forgetting his lifelong knowledge that U-3 could not speak.

'AM-12, What's happening?'

'We are following your instructions, Sir,' AM-12 said. 'The instructions of the *Die Master*. When the memory of your old life returns, it is time for your mind to be *cleared*. We have followed this procedure many times before.'

Although the Young Master struggled, the robots were too strong for him. They held his arms and legs as they lowered an evil-smelling mask onto his face.

The Young Master awoke to find the sun streaming in through the window. AM-12 entered the room.

'Another fine morning, Sir,' AM-12 said. 'Soon it will be time for breakfast, and then time to run the trains, and this afternoon we will all assemble for cricket on the south lawn.'

Chapter Sixteen

The doorbell echoed shrilly around the inside of Crystal House. Louise started, not expecting Exeter to call so early. She had only just got up. But she was looking forward to his visit, to showing him around Crystal House, before they waited together for the stranger to call.

She rolled the front door aside but saw no one out there.

'Exeter?' she called.

Then a balding man with a black cloak and a staff like an old-time preacher appeared, making a high-pitched whining in his throat.

'I have lost my flock!' he wailed. 'Good lady, I beseech thee. Aid me, for I have lost my flock.'

Louise stepped back and slid the door shut again. Only when the comforting clicks of the locks echoed around her did she realise that this was another strange caller, but much earlier than before.

She put her ear to the door but could hear nothing. She wanted Exeter to come now so that he would see for himself one of the weird people who plagued her doorstep.

She grimaced with irritation but then felt that the strangers had now called so regularly that she felt somehow more confident about facing them, as if her fear was becoming familiarity. None of the callers had actually tried to force their way into the house or threatened her, so perhaps they were not so dangerous after all.

Again, Louise put her ear to the door. This time she heard a mumbling, as if the man was talking to himself. She unlatched the bolts again and rolled the door open a crack.

'My prayers are answered,' the man said.

'Who are you?'

'I am the leader of the *Sect*. But I have lost my flock!'

'Where did you see them last?'

The man began to beat at the ground with his stick like a madman.

'It is not for thee to ask me questions, Lady!' he yelled.

'So how can I help you?'

'Let me into Crystal House.'

'And how will that help?'

'There are things within thy dwelling that will help me. I foresee that when I am permitted to cross thy threshold, my flock will return. And then thou wilt be blessed and wilt wonder at thy fullness.'

Louise looked at his hands. They were the same tiny hands, and they held an unused little notebook. She knew she was right. All the strange callers were just this one person.

'You look like a madman to me,' Louise said. 'It's you who's been calling here every day, dressing up and pretending to be that man in the car, the bread man, the baker, and the little girl from the crash. You're not funny, and I don't like it.'

'Nay... nay!' The man looked uncertainly into her face now. She almost expected to see the face of a friend, someone she knew, playing a joke. But his face was still unknown.

'I'm going to close the door now,' she said. 'You can dress up as something else tomorrow, but I've had enough of you for today.'

'A glass of water...?'

Louise slammed the door shut. A few moments later she slid it open again, but now he was gone.

When the doorbell rang again, it was Exeter, carrying a picnic hamper.

'You're too late, Louise said. 'He's already been.'

'Shall we take a walk around on the hill?' Exeter suggested. 'I've brought some lunch.'

So Louise locked up the house and went with Exeter van Hoyland out to the main road, from where they followed a narrow footpath uphill. It led them between high hedges of diseased wood, up to a bald, wide-open space, right on top of the hill, with a view of the sea. Nearby, Louise saw a square stone tower and then, behind her, a square white chimney among the trees.

'That chimney's yours,' Exeter said. 'That's Crystal House.'

Louise stared at the chimney as it shimmered in the warm air, then looked at the sea.

'You can't see that water from Crystal House,' she said. 'All my vile trees are in the way. Why do you think my trees are so sick?'

'Why is anything the way it is on this hill? It's all peculiar up here. When people like the Superheroes have lived in one place for so long, it's bound to make that place a little unusual.'

Exeter took out something that looked like a wide writing pen, pressed a button, and showed her a tiny display of numbers.

'This shows the radiation,' he said. 'Safe, but quite high. A lot of the places up on this hill have their own atomic power.'

'Is it safe?'

'Oh, yes, the government will have made sure of that.'

Exeter opened the hamper and laid out a red cloth on the grass. Anywhere else, and this would have been idyllic. The saturated colours on this cloudless day made the scene look like something from an old film. They were alone, on a red island in a vast expanse of green. Louise caught sight of the gold of her wig. Then the blue dome of the sky above her felt close, like a lid. Every shadow among the trees was a deep and impenetrable black.

'What else do you know about this hill?' Louise asked.

'A lot of the Superheroes had their homes up here. There were houses on the hill before the Heroes came, but they bought them up one by one and took them over.'

'So which Heroes lived on the hill?'

'Golden Man and Glinda.'

'Sound nice.'

'They are. Those two still live here. And then there was Theo Banks, who was the Die Master. He was a Superhero who could never be killed. Something really weird happened to him. He began to grow both older and younger at the same time.

'T-Man had his problems too. He never lived here, but when he first used his powers, something odd began to happen to his body. He seemed to get eaten away a little bit every time he used them. He overcame that somehow. He used his powers on himself to fix the problem, I guess.'

'That's another of the Superhero houses, over there,' Exeter said, pointing to a wall in the distance. 'I think the Criterion used to live there. He's dead, so I expect it's just empty now, waiting in probate, like a lot of the houses up here.'

'Why would it be in probate?'

'Because there's a lot of interference by the government in the ownership of these houses, especially now that President Rayonier's in power. After any of the Heroes die, nowadays the government always challenges the wills, just in case there's any technology or special tools left behind that can be used.'

'Then I wonder how Crystal House came so quickly and easily to me?'

'You were lucky. President Rayonier's such a bandit.'

After eating, they took a slightly different path back to Crystal House. They ended up following a high wall, and now another building came into sight ahead. It was a chapel, but of an unusual design. It was built in two halves, split by the wall.

'The Chapel of Super Prayer,' Exeter said. 'It was built to petition the Superheroes. People came here to pray, to have their problems solved, because sometimes the Superheroes came and listened to them from the other half of the chapel - beyond the wall.'

They were right by the entrance now. Several cars were parked nearby, and they heard a murmuring from inside the building. Louise looked at some stone figures set into alcoves on the walls, but they were not Superheroes. She read an inscription. The figures represented the world's woes. 'Pestilence' was one.

It took a while for her eyes to adjust to the gloom. She looked at the man in the pulpit, remembering the leader of the 'Sect' who had called at Crystal House, and tried to work out whether it was the same man, but she could not tell. She shut her eyes and saw stars as the man in the pulpit beseeched any possible Superheroes beyond the wall. He was praying to them to avoid a war.

Chapter Seventeen

In the morning, while bathing the Young Master, the robots unthinkingly held his head underwater for several seconds, and he nearly drowned. It was as if, without AM-10, they did not know how to look after him properly.

These days, the robots mostly left the boy alone, and he was free to roam the grounds at will. He explored all the lawns and the trees. He longed to explore further away. At first he found every side of his world bounded by the Wall, but then he discovered a wooden frame the robots used to clean the house windows. It was easy then. He stepped onto the top of the Wall and jumped down from the other side, with no thought of how he might return.

He came to the road and, beyond the road, among the trees, found another wall. He climbed that and then came to more trees, but these looked diseased. Presently he came to a big white structure, another house, but so strong-looking that he thought it must be a place where someone very scared would live.

An unexpected part of the building popped open, and a woman came out. She wore a purple cloak and a mask that covered the top part of her face. She was beautiful.

'Hello, Theo,' the Moon Queen said. 'What's bothering you now?'

The Young Master had no idea who she was or what she was talking about. She was friendly, although she would not let him touch her, and she took him into the house. Soon he found himself sitting in a huge seat, which she called the 'Moon Chair'.

'I'll call you Theo,' she said, 'because that's your real name. You aren't the 'Young Master' in my house. I see that your robots have taken your memory again.'

The Young Master looked around the room, at the beautiful *Moon Queen* with her exasperated smile.

'You were never as bad as the rest of them, Theo,' she said, 'though you were bad enough. Do you know how sick I got of just about everyone in the world lusting after me all the time?' her voice trailed off as the Young

Master, uninterested in what she was saying, stared at the enormous silver women who stood silently around the room.

'You used to know them, Theo, and they belong to you. You can stay here for the afternoon. You probably need a rest from your own house for a while.'

She gave him some sweets from a jar. Then she began to amuse herself by showing him over Crystal House. She showed how a switch inside a gleaming chrome console table could make model dummies of herself spring up from underground, outside in the garden, to deflect an intruder's attack.

The Young Master was fascinated by the tremendous steel blast shutters that could be made to swing out from hidden pockets and cover the windows. The Moon Queen was clever as well as beautiful.

'I don't usually encourage visitors, Theo, but you may come here whenever you like,' she said with a smile. 'Just come into the garden and I'll meet you. Now that your mentor robot is gone, I feel that I have some small responsibility towards you.'

The Young Master wondered if that meant the Moon Queen loved him. She let him sit again in the Moon Chair, and he watched as a wall panel slid back to reveal a brass calculator that showed the times when the moon would rise. She told him that when the moon was high, she would sit in that chair to watch it cross the night sky. That sounded like the greatest thing the Young Master had ever heard. From here, on a clear night, she said, it was possible to see for a hundred miles.

She made them a meal, and, as they ate, she turned a switch on a box, and a TV picture appeared. A man there began speaking.

'Today, we report an unexpected attack - by Supervillain Morthwil - on the home of retired Superhero Conway Johns,' the man said, although the Young Master just watched the image and paid no attention to the words. He stared, fascinated, at the scenes of destruction that were shown. The newsman's face came back, but the Young Master was now looking at the texture of his skin. It was more like his own than it was like the Moon Queen's, which looked drier and looser despite her beauty. The Young Master supposed, unaware of how he knew, that it meant she was old. She wasn't paying him any attention anymore. She was also staring at the TV.

'I'm sorry, Theo, but it's time for you to go,' she said. 'Forget what I said before. You can't come back here. This is not a safe house for you now. I want you to go back home and stay there. Tell your robots not to let you go beyond your grounds. Tell them *Code Red*. Remember that, Theo. *Code Red*. They will understand what you mean.'

The Young Master was disappointed at being told he could not return to see the beautiful woman. He had just made a new friend, and now she was sending him away. She kept talking to him about danger and 'Code Red' as she led him out through the secret door, away from her house, back through the trees until, finally, they reached the Wall. She lifted him up so that he could reach the top.

'Listen, Theo,' she said. 'We're not safe anymore. Remember. Tell your robots. *Code Red*.

'One more thing. Try not to let your robots see how much you know. You need to keep your wits about you now.'

The Young Master looked back, bewildered. He tried to tell her about his favourite games to extend their time together, but she just said to jump down the other side.

As he approached the house, a robot came towards him. It was U-3.

'*Code Red*,' the Young Master said.

U-3 immediately gripped his arm and began to rush towards the house. But as he was dragged along, the Young Master saw a yellow glow among the trees. He knew what that was. It was the light of the moon beginning to rise.

Chapter Eighteen

At about 3 am, Exeter van Hoyland found that he was unable to sleep. As usual when this happened, he went to his car to have a drive. He went down to Crescent City, driving along the lanes.

The road was interrupted by roadblocks and police cars. They made him wait and took his name, and he saw some shadowy official cars drive by, heading the other way. He drove to the coast and looked out to sea in the night.

Then, back past the roadblock, back at the Peacock as it began to get light, he saw the news on TV. President Rayonier had been to Crescent City. He had visited the hill and gone to the house of Glinda and the Golden Man.

Why, Exeter had wondered, had Rayonier not asked T-Man for help? T-Man, the most powerful Superhero of them all? Then he thought of the answer. Rayonier *had* gone to

T-Man but had been refused, had probably not even been allowed into the Superhero's house.

Then the TV showed the aged Golden Man with Glinda by his side, flying away towards the South, then General Cranston clambering aboard a huge aircraft with his troops to fly that way too. But then it showed terrible flickering lights among the clouds and the sound of thunder. The newsman looked grave and said that the Golden Man and Glinda had disappeared.

Exeter watched the news all morning. President Rayonier declared a state of emergency, in readiness for a counter-attack. There were long, anxious TV interviews with military personnel. Generals gave their analysis of the situation, but it was as if what they were speaking of was a natural disaster that had somehow arisen, with nobody to blame.

Exeter thought of his sister, the nurse, down there in the Oil Lands. She normally wrote to him every week, but for some time now he had not received a letter. Then he thought of Louise. He had to make sure she was alright. He went to the receptionist by the main door and told her that he would be gone for a while.

As Exeter approached Crystal House, he saw a shape among the trees like the figure of a person. He still did not know what to think of Louise's tales of mysterious callers. Then he saw that the figure was Louise herself.

'Hi, Exeter!' He heard her words through the still air. 'Thanks for coming. My caller hasn't been yet. I wouldn't be surprised if he doesn't come because I gave him such a talking-to last time.'

Now Exeter was within a few feet of her, but she must have seen something in his face even from that far away.

'You don't believe me, do you? You don't think anyone really comes?'

'Sorry, Louise. I've been preoccupied with what's happening in the South. Did you see the news this morning?'

'I don't watch it.'

'The Golden Man and Glinda flew down there in the night, and I think they're dead. The situation has all changed, and I think that possibly Morthwil is on their side.'

'Morthwil's evil, Exeter. Remember what he did to Conway Johns' house. Well, it's nice of you to come and see me anyway. But I'm sorry, Exeter. Because I'm still a bit scared, I'm not going to let even you inside the house.'

'That's OK, Louise.'

'You wait then, and I'll get us some coffee.'

Louise left the door open behind her. She trusted him not to follow her inside.

Exeter stood there in the early morning light. Then he turned to look back along the driveway, the way a stranger would come. He crunched at the gravel with his foot and saw a tiny cloud of dust rise by his shoe. Then he heard the sound of footsteps.

Incredibly, an important-looking military general was making his way up towards the house. He looked just like the ones on the TV. In fact, it was - it was General Cranston! Exeter stared at the medals and the gold braid as Cranston's uniform gleamed in the morning sun. Cranston stopped, a few feet away.

'Crystal House?'

'Yes, this is Crystal House.'

'Residence of the Moon Queen? I must gain entry immediately.'

But Exeter remembered having seen Cranston board a plane. By now he should be thousands of miles away, flying down to the South.

'I'm afraid the Moon Queen is dead,' Exeter said, 'and her niece owns Crystal House now.'

'OK.'

Cranston stepped forward as if to go into the house, but then Exeter saw what was happening. He was letting his disbelief of Louise's tales get the better of him. This kind of thing was exactly what she was frightened of.

'Wait!' Exeter said, moving his body to block the doorway. 'Just wait, will you?'

Cranston glared.

'Just wait until the new owner comes back, if you don't mind, General Cranston. She won't be long. Then she can let you into the house herself.'

'I will enter Crystal House now.' Cranston took another step forward. Exeter got ready to yell into the house, to warn Louise. He suddenly realised what it must be like to be her, alone here at the mercy of the doorbell every day. He felt the general's hands grip his arm, as though to try and move him to one side, but they were tiny hands, not strong enough to move Exeter at all.

'Perhaps I will call at another time,' Cranston snorted. He turned and began to march back down the drive. Exeter stared after him until he'd gone out of sight. Then Louise came back from inside the house carrying two cups. She looked happy, but Exeter could not smile back.

'He's been,' was all he could say, and he suddenly realised that he was shaking.

Chapter Nineteen

The Young Master tried to stem the flow of blood, but at the same time he was fascinated by the thick liquid that oozed from his knee. He had been trying to climb the Wall again. He felt that a robot should have come to tend him, but now they were not such able guardians. They had guarded him closely the night he had said 'Code Red', but after that the alarm had gradually died back down.

The Young Master looked up at the Wall again. The convenient wooden frame he had used last time had been taken away, but after several practice attempts, higher and higher, he reached the top, and then the jump down the other side was easy.

Walking among the undergrowth that surrounded Crystal House, the Young Master thought of his friend, the old lady, the Moon Queen, about how he hoped she would be pleased to see him again.

As he approached the gleaming white fortress, he called out, 'It's Theo!' He used the unfamiliar name, the one the lady liked to use, but no one answered and no one came. The house looked as silent as a tomb. He called out again, but then he remembered the secret door, the way an unexpected part of the house had opened out the last time he had been here.

At first he could not find the place because it was so well hidden. The wall and the window section that opened looked like the last place anyone would put a door. If he had not already known of its existence, he would never have guessed it was there. He planted his hands on the rough concrete and pushed, trying to slide it sideways. It was only when he remembered his skills at climbing, when he tried to grip and pull the surface outwards, that he felt movement. There was an almost imperceptible sliding sound as the secret door began to move, and then the gap was open. He stepped up into the house straight away because he knew he would be welcome.

He called out *It's Theo!* again, and then, as he rounded a corner, saw one of the enormous silver women standing silently in the gloom. He stopped. Suddenly the old woman's house felt like her private place, where he might not be welcome after all. He walked through the corridors until he found the Moon Chair in its central room, and stared out at the tops of the sickly trees through the tall window there, but after a while he began to feel such a trespasser that he decided to go home.

The next day the Young Master led robot U-3 to the Wall. He had hatched a plan the night before, and, although U-3 was not the ideal companion for it, the robot was still the one the Young Master knew best. As U-3 stood watching, the boy showed the robot how he had learned to climb over. He waved back at U-3, jumped down the other side, and waited. Then the sound he had hoped for came. U-3 had found a way to follow him.

'Well done, U-3,' he said as the robot approached. 'Now come and help me find her.'

He led U-3 across the road, over the other wall, and into the grounds of Crystal House, the robot following him through the undergrowth. Then U-3 marched forward quickly, held onto his arm, and pulled him back.

The Young Master saw why. A man was standing in front of Crystal House, dressed all in black with a big square hat. The Young Master crouched close to U-3. If there was a man at Crystal House, it meant that the Moon Queen might have returned. The man stood, staring into the trees for a while, and then moved slowly around to the other side of the house. The Young Master decided to follow him. The boy crept silently among the trees with U-3 right next to him and saw something black and gleaming on the drive - a big car. More men in black were standing about nearby, and then they went up to the door and into the house. Perhaps the Moon Queen had asked them to enter. The Young Master looked on, fascinated, wondering what would happen next.

Finally, the men reappeared. Now they were walking very slowly, carrying a long, shiny box, shapely in its construction. It looked quite elegant. They opened the back of the car and loaded the box inside. The Young Master wondered what they were taking away. He had hoped they might be carrying out one of the silver women, but the box was not big enough for one of those. And then the Young Master realised just what it was that the box was just the right size to carry, and he knew he was never going to see the Moon Queen again.

Exeter van Hoyland stared at the TV. Helicopters hovered over the sea, winching down loops of cable. They had found human remains, the severed lower half of the Golden Man.

The helicopter's rotor whirled as it took the weight. There was no trace of Glinda.

How loyally they rushed off to do Rayonier's bidding, Exeter thought. They must have thought it was like a return to the old days, to get the call, to have a mission. The helicopter dumped the dead hips and legs clumsily onto the beach.

Chapter Twenty

Some days later, alone, the Young Master went again to the grounds of Crystal House. Now it was as if having seen the Moon Queen's body being carried away meant the final end for this place. The boy imagined a future where the sickly trees grew slowly closer to the house and spread their branches across the windows, the trunks with their grotesque swellings creeping gradually over everything.

He passed a tree that had split open all by itself, revealing diseased red heartwood that looked like blood. He stopped, scared. He suddenly imagined the same forces that had blighted the trees at work within his own body, but somehow suspended, like a tiny nightmare, waiting for him. To escape from that nightmare, he looked up to the top of the house, where there was a high platform like a chimney. The poisoned branches almost reached up there.

He remembered the Moon Queen's face and her beauty despite her great age. He felt as if the old woman had promised him something, and that, even though she had gone away, he may still find it.

He began to find patches where the trees looked almost normal, but then there came areas where their sickly growths became fantastic and impenetrable. He saw a shimmering in the air, a cloud of flying insects, and followed them, almost like following an aerial highway, to a place where the trees looked their worst. A deathly sweet odour came. He passed a fat buttress that supported part of the house's massive wall, and saw an armoured conduit curving up to the building from somewhere beneath the ground. A faint humming came. Around the conduit, the biology of the trees had become completely confused, with painful bulbous growths. It looked almost as if new organisms were trying to form themselves from the raw material of the wood in an unnatural living carpentry. Swollen branches bent to the ground to become a sweet soup that formed scum-encrusted pools. Skulls of dead animals surrounded that place.

But the insects had made it their feeding ground. They alighted on the sickly pools, some of their bodies forming the lumpy crust, but those which had survived the deadliness there returned to spread this disease more widely among the rest of the trees. The Young Master crept towards the grim little pool, his throat tightening. He knelt and stared at the liquid, attracted to it like the insects, becoming intoxicated by its sticky sweetness.

Then he heard a sound, a rush of tyres, and a slammed car door. Another car had come to the front of the house. Was it the Moon Queen, come back? He stepped away from the pool, suddenly feeling proper revulsion for it. Shock filled his eyes as he ran around the house, the fear making him hate the touch of the twigs and leaves as he brushed among them.

A yellow car with a little square sign on the roof and writing on the doors was parked on the drive. A man and a woman were in there, but the woman was bald and held false hair in her hand. The man got out and opened the car door for her. He was trying not to look as the woman put her hair back on. The man carried some bags up to the front door and then hurried back to the car while the woman used a key. The front door slid aside. The Young Master watched as the woman stood in the doorway.

The Young Master needed to think about all he had just seen. He ran home, ran up to his house across the familiar, healthy lawns. He needed to return to the security of his robots now.

'U-3!' he called as he ran towards the front door, 'U-3, I need you!'

U-3 appeared in the hallway, but now he looked different - not changed in himself, but changed in how the Young Master saw him. The feeling of security the boy wanted did not come.

Chapter Twenty-One

Louise awoke early, feeling as if she had not slept at all, and prepared herself for the strange caller to come yet again. She went to the Moon Room and stood there, looking at the big chair in the centre, then took the lift up to the top of the chimney structure above the roof. After a while, she descended to the house again. Then she went through all the corridors, walking among the statues of silver women that towered above her.

The doorbell echoed. She wondered what disguise the caller would be wearing today. She unlocked the latches and slid the door aside. She did not recognise the man there at first because too many years had passed.

'Louise? Hi. It's me, Harry Wildwood.'

And then Louise knew who he was: Harry Wildwood, her friend from her childhood days on the border, a time of her life now almost forgotten.

'Harry, I haven't seen you for *years*.'

'Great to find you, Louise. Great that you're here. I thought I'd come to see you!'

'How did you know where I live?'

'I live in Crescent City too. I didn't know your aunt had been the Moon Queen. You never told me, all that time we used to read comics when we were kids!'

Harry looked up at Crystal House.

'What's it like inside?'

'Just as scary,' Louise laughed.

'So this is where the Moon Queen lived. She was the best. She was really beautiful.'

Is there anyone who didn't lust after my aunt? Louise asked herself. She paused. She had been about to invite Harry inside but now she said, 'Show me your hands.'

The smile left Harry's face as he held out his hands for Louise to examine. They were normal-sized, so Louise nodded, again about to invite Harry inside, but then he spoke again.

'I met Jeff,' he said. 'That's how I found out that you lived here now.'

Louise bit her tongue. Something odd was going on.

'Aren't you going to show me inside?' Harry asked. But Louise suddenly recalled an image in one of the comics Exeter had shown her, where the Moon Queen had been fighting for her life.

'Why are you living here, Louise? Why are you staying in this house?' Harry asked. 'Why not just sell it? You'd make a fortune selling a place like this. But while I'm here, I'd be grateful if you let me take a look around inside.'

'Why do you keep asking about the house, Harry? And when did you meet Jeff?'

'He just told me that you'd split up. He asked me to make sure you were OK.'

Louise stared at him.

'Did he tell you what he did to me?'

Harry just looked confused. Louise tore off her wig to show him her blasted scalp. Her forehead itched. She scratched at the join between her old and new skin.

'I didn't know,' Harry said, staring. 'He didn't tell me much. So are you going to show me inside the house?'

'I don't let anyone into my house.'

'Are you OK, Louise?'

'No, I'm not, Harry. I don't like it that you've been sent here by Jeff. I have to think about that.' Tears came to her eyes as she felt her scalp rage with pain. 'Harry,' she whispered, 'perhaps you'd better go?'

'OK.' Harry turned away. He set off down the drive without another word. As she watched him go, Louise hoped he would look back, but he did not.

She stood alone on the doorstep as the wind blustered through the sick trees. There was a new shape that was out of place over there, but her eyes had passed on before she could recognise it. In the corner of her eye, she thought she saw a tiny face look at her then disappear.

She felt herself grabbed, hard, by her fear and forced back into the house. She rolled the door shut, activated the latches, and only when she heard the bolts thump home did her mind let her recall the most important news: *Jeff knew she was in Crystal House!*

Chapter Twenty-Two

The next morning, the doorbell rang while Louise still lay slumped in bed. Was it the caller again? Or perhaps it was already Jeff, 'come to see if she was OK'. Perhaps Harry had already spoken to him and told him she lived alone here, and so Jeff thought he could come and...

She got up and switched on the TV, loud, to drown out the sound of the doorbell, but a news bulletin came on. She saw the severed lower half of the Golden Man rising from the sea, with the roaring helicopter taking the weight, and then the rest of him being dumped on the beach. She turned the TV off, recalling Conway Johns speaking of his attack by Morthwil and mentioning Crystal House.

She couldn't stay here. She was setting herself up as a target. *Get out now, sell it, and find someplace else to live!* she told herself. That was what Harry had suggested. *First of all, I will take Exeter up on his offer of a room at the Peacock.*

But she collapsed back into her bed, exhausted, and did not awake again until late in the afternoon as the sky was darkening. She was about to close the blinds when she saw the moon shining above the trees. It was too late to go to the Peacock now. Louise began planning her move, letting herself get lost in the practical details of it. She did not have many things here. She would be able to find somewhere to rent while staying at the Peacock. She began to feel better, as if the decision to leave had liberated her. Then she opened the wardrobe and saw Exeter's gift, the costume of the Moon Queen. She had put it away there carefully the first night, not caring for it much.

She took it out and looked at it, admiring it properly for the first time. She had been scared of it up until now, but, as she would be leaving this place soon and so leaving everything about her aunt behind, her fear was reduced. She laid out the costume on her bed and took off her wig. She thought about how the Superheroes were people with extra gifts while she herself no longer even had a proper head, but the smooth Moon Queen face mask would fit her better than it would fit most women because she would not have to tidy away her hair. Standing in front of the mirror, she carefully flattened the skull cap down around her ears. It was far more comfortable than her wig, and it fitted perfectly. She rolled the mask down over the top half of her face. Looking out from the large eyeholes, she saw the reflection of her mouth twitch sardonically as she wondered what the hell she was doing. But then, as she continued to watch herself, she saw that she was beautiful.

She picked up the large purple cape and clipped it on, almost laughing as she held up the main body stocking. If Exeter thought she was going to wear that skin-tight jumpsuit he had another think coming. But she remembered that Exeter had not encouraged her to wear the costume at all. That had been her own idea.

She admired herself in the mirror until she decided to put on the body stocking after all. It was very tight, made to fit whoever had previously worn it - in a film, she remembered. She paced up and down the room, getting used to the tight grip of the costume around her waist, and then decided to dare something. Despite the fact she now planned to move, Crystal House still belonged to her today.

Louise opened the door to the main part of the house and looked ahead along the corridor. She reminded herself that this house was one of the most secure places in the world, and that no one at all apart from herself had entered here since she had arrived. Her elegant costume reflected in the curved bodies of the silver women as she crept silently through the corridors and saw the glow from the doorway to the Moon Room. Tonight this was where she belonged. The moon itself hung outside the window, casting its pale light. Branches from the sick trees reached out for the delicate sphere, but it hovered above them, free.

Facing away from her, the Moon Chair towered in the centre of the room. Louise suddenly felt a presence, as if someone was already sitting there. Her heart almost stopped.

'Hello?' she whispered.

She crept forward, around the chair, but as the front gradually came into view there was no one. Then she was sitting in the chair, and her sight was filled with the clouds racing across the moon. She felt almost inhuman. She thought of her dead aunt, Agnes.

'Hello,' she said again, in case her spirit was still present, 'I'm sorry I didn't know anything about you.'

She did not see the child outside among the trees, or his mouth broadening into a smile. She did not see him even as he moved closer, out from the cover of the undergrowth, no longer caring if he was seen, right up to the glass. Louise just stared at the billowing sky. All her life, she had closed the curtains when it got dark, but now the hurrying moon made her feel she was living in a new world, where anything was possible. She finally saw the tiny face watching her from the corner of the window.

The Young Master looked in. He had been wrong when he'd thought the Moon Queen was dead. He raised his arm and waved while, inside the house, Louise even raised her own arm to wave back.

Chapter Twenty-Three

The next morning, sitting in the Moon Chair during the night seemed like a drunken dream. Louise remembered properly that she had to sell Crystal House. She remembered Morthwil. He was the reason why. And the little face at the window - who had *that* been? She shuddered at the recollection.

She looked into the Moon Room, trying to work out exactly what had come over her the night before. Then she felt a slight pulse of air, as if someone had opened a door or a window elsewhere in the house.

Jeff! she thought. But that was insane.

She ran to the front door, but it was still shut, and the bolts were all in place. Could there be a window open somewhere? It was a big house, but surely she knew it all by now? She began to work out how she could systematically check. She should start at the top...

Footsteps.

She stood completely still, trying to remember how much noise she'd made when she'd run to check the front door. She had not taken care to be silent. The footsteps came closer.

'Miss Bale?' the Young Master called out.

Louise saw the face from the previous night. A boy with long fair hair, wearing old-fashioned clothes. The first person who had entered Crystal House since Louise had been here. He had not come through the front door - he had just appeared in here. Louise's mind reeled with the impossibility of it. Was there another way into Crystal House?

'Who are you?'

'You know me already. I'm Theo Banks.'

But then, as he came closer, the Young Master saw that Louise was not the woman he recognised as his friend.

'You're the bald one,' Theo said, 'the one with no hair.' he looked disappointed. 'I came to see Miss Bale.'

'That's me. I'm Miss Bale.'

'No.'

Louise realised who he was looking for.

'You mean *Agnes* Bale. She was my aunt. But now she's dead, and this is my house. It's private. How did you get in here?'

'I know the way in.'

'Let me see your hands!' Louise demanded.

Theo's hands were small but were not the hands of the strange caller.

'So, you knew my aunt?' Louise said.

'Yes. You look like her.'

'Was she your friend?

Theo nodded.

'Listen, Theo, I need you to show me how you got into my house. You can't just walk in here whenever you like.'

Louise had expected Theo to show her something like a small window or a ventilator somewhere that only he could squeeze through, and so she was puzzled when he stood next to a big sealed window next to the back stairs. He just touched the wall in a certain place, and a large section of it moved quickly and silently aside, leaving a wide, open-air view of the garden. Now there was a huge, gaping hole in the side of the house. Theo stepped calmly out onto the grass while Louise shivered in the air that blew into the house, the draught she had felt from the Moon Room.

'How does this close? How does it *lock?*' she demanded.

Theo came back in.

'There is no lock,' he said as he reached up, touched the wall, and closed the hole again. 'It will open quite quickly. Miss Bale said it was important to be able to leave the house right away, in case her enemies ever got in.'

Louise shuddered. As soon as this boy had gone, she would seal up that death trap right away.

Dazed, she let Theo show her all over Crystal House. He knew far more about it than she did and talked to her quite happily, only falling silent when they came near any of the silver women. Louise looked up as they passed one, seeing the pair of them reflected in the statue's silver side. Theo deliberately looked away.

He knew how to operate the lift to the roof, and he knew the Moon Room and the Moon Chair. He showed her the control switch in the chrome console table that made a full-size dummy of the Moon Queen spring up from underground in the garden. That was the oddest thing she had ever seen. As she looked out at the figure, watching its cape move softly in the breeze, she almost felt as if her aunt was alive again.

Theo knew how to circle quickly around inside the house, up the main stairs and then down the back staircase by the secret door. Her aunt had once told him it was important to know how to do that.

In one of the rooms, he went across to the fireplace and reached up to take an urn from the mantelpiece. Louise watched, puzzled, as he brought it across to her. She half expected to find her aunt's ashes in there. She took the urn from him and lifted the lid, but found just sweets inside. Her aunt's store of sweets, possibly especially for Theo. She offered him one, and then he smiled up at her as if his friend the Moon Queen had returned.

'I'm nothing like my aunt.' Louise said. I'm not a Hero or a Heroine.'

'You look like her.'

'I'm not the Moon Queen. She's gone forever. Everything has changed here. What you saw last night was only me, dressing up.

And another thing is, I'm not going to be staying on in Crystal House. I'm going to sell it. I'll be moving away, and then someone else is going to come and live here, and they won't want you to just walk in. Don't do that again.

'Where do *you* live, Theo?'

'Not far away. You can come and visit me.'

After Theo had gone, Louise tried to work out how to seal up the secret door, but there was no visible lock, and there seemed to be no way of doing it. So that evening she spent a lot of effort single-handedly shifting a large sideboard through from one of the rooms and stood it in front of there.

Chapter Twenty-Four

Louise cleaned around the house all morning, ready for when the estate agent came.

He arrived at the correct time, to the second, as if he'd come slightly early and been waiting outside. His bright red car was parked on the drive behind him.

'Miss Bale?' he said. 'Pleased to meet you!

'Ah, a very spacious house, and on the hill. We'll have no trouble finding a buyer for you!' He looked around the hallway appreciatively as soon as he came in.

Louise hadn't meant for him to enter the house yet. After Theo, this estate agent was the second person ever to come into the Moon Queen's house since Louise had been living here, but it was as if Theo had broken her defences. The estate agent began looking around, taking measurements of the rooms with his little device, as if this was just a normal house, as if anyone could come in here and live a normal life.

'The walls are unusually thick,' he said. Louise just nodded. The estate agent indicated one of the silver women.

'You'll be taking these with you?'

'I want to get rid of them. They're not important. I just want to sell. You'll already know that this is one of the old Superhero houses. That might be the reason those statues are here. My aunt was the Moon Queen.'

'I did suspect something of the sort, as you are on the hill. But in that case, one thing I must ask, Miss Bale, is whether your title to the house is completely in order. The Superheroes' entitlement to the land they held up here was sometimes legally rather uncertain. When they arrived they didn't always follow the... niceties. You'll have to make sure that your ownership is sound. The government also sometimes takes an interest in these properties.'

'I got all the documents when I inherited it. They've been checked legally, and they look OK to me.'

'Good. It might be an idea to have an extra check with your lawyer though, just to make sure. I'm not being funny with you, Miss Bale. Any estate agent would tell you the same about a house like this.'

He continued measuring the rooms. After Theo, this visit had completely broken Crystal House's spell.

But then, when the estate agent went into the Moon Room and saw the Moon Chair, he began to look uneasy. A cloud in front of the sun made the room suddenly look dark. He scratched the back of his neck.

'What's this, exactly?' he asked, touching the arm of the chair.

'The Moon Chair,' Louise said. 'It was my aunt's, the Moon Queen's.'

The estate agent's eyes darted from side to side.

'There's nothing to be afraid of,' Louise said, but that seemed to make it worse for the man, as if the possibility of fear had now been brought out in the open.

'I... I can't put a value on this house!'

'Why not? Do you need to look around some more?'

'No. This type of property is not my speciality. It may be that the only way you could sell this house is for... for total redevelopment. Yes, that's it. Total redevelopment.' The estate agent left the Moon Room, and Louise heard him scurrying back towards the front door. The light changed as the sun came out from behind the cloud again, and Louise saw a single strand of cobweb that arched right across the room, where she had just been cleaning a few minutes ago. The cobweb ended in mid-air, right by where the estate agent had been standing.

'The front door is unlocked, I hope?' he called back nervously. Louise went after him. He had a hold of the handle inside the door but couldn't open it, even though Louise had not slid the bolts shut.

'Don't keep me here! I have another appointment!' The estate agent jerked at the handle.

Louise rolled the door back quite easily. The estate agent ran to his car and stalled the engine. He restarted it and drove away, engine roaring, in a spray of gravel.

Shortly afterwards, another man came to the door, an older, more experienced-looking man. He wore a faded green suit.

'I must apologise for my colleague who was just here,' he said. 'He's new at our office and a little inexperienced. Perhaps I may take a little look around this house?' He stepped over the threshold.

'Very nice house. Great location,' he said as he took out a small, clean notebook, 'and a good stand of trees.'

'What are these?' he said, looking at the silver women.

'I don't know. They were here when I got here, like everything else in the house.'

'I hope you don't mind,' the man said, 'but I've been looking at houses since early this morning. Could I have a cup of coffee?'

'Good idea,' Louise said. 'I'll have one too.'

'I'll continue looking around the ground floor while you prepare it, shall I? I'll just go from room to room.'

Somehow it took Louise a long time to make the coffee, as if she was in a dream, or as if the sound of boiling water had become hypnotic. When the coffee was ready, she found that she couldn't hear the man downstairs anymore.

'Hello?' she called out, because he hadn't even told her his name.

Where was he? She looked into the Moon Room. It was empty.

She explored all the downstairs rooms. Perhaps the man had needed to go back outside, to look at the exterior, before putting a value on the house. But she was not convinced he had gone out.

She searched throughout the ground floor, through all the huge rooms, past fireplaces, past silver women, but the ground floor was empty. Then she went to the back stairs and crept silently back to the upper floor.

If the second estate agent was still in the house, he must have come up here. Louise looked into the rooms in the main part of the upstairs, but they were all empty. She even pressed the button for the lift to the roof, but the rumble the lift door made as it opened was too loud for her to not have noticed it before. That meant the man was still somewhere on this floor. The only place left where he could be now was in her personal rooms - her own bathroom, kitchen, and bedroom.

Her footsteps sounded incredibly loud as she went into the kitchen. The coffees were still there. At first, she could not believe he had been there, but then she saw the small, clean notebook on the table. She remembered him taking it from his pocket. Then she suddenly saw an image of his tiny hands, heard his voice casually convincing her that he was genuine and asking for a coffee.

Louise watched the sun shining on the trees outside as she stood in the kitchen, trying to make herself acknowledge just how serious it was that the weird stranger with the tiny hands had finally entered her house. Although her mind felt sluggish, it told her that the only place left that the man could possibly be was in her bedroom.

The door to the bedroom was slightly ajar, and a faint sound came from behind it, like someone breathing heavily. Louise peered in and saw the back of the man. He was surrounded by a cloud of insects, but what worried Louise more was that he was kneeling on the floor, pawing at her bed with his hands, caressing the bedclothes, and squeezing the pillows to his face. Then he must have heard her, because he turned around. Now he wore a mask and was dressed in a green costume.

'I'm sorry to have deceived you,' he said. 'My name is Hyperion, and I was a friend of your aunt's.'

Chapter Twenty-Five

Exeter didn't take Louise's story of the visit by Hyperion as seriously as she had expected. He laughed out loud when she told him that he had been all the strange callers.

'But it was terrible,' Louise complained. 'He just said he had to go in there, in his costume, to 'her' bedroom. And then he had this disgusting cloud of flies buzzing around him. How creepy is that? And he was *feeling* my bed. Then he just said 'thank you,' and left.'

'I'm sorry,' Exeter laughed. 'I know it's not funny. But at least now you know your visits by strange callers are over. He's been into Crystal House now, paid his respects.'

'But when he was... caressing my bed, it was like some kind of sex thing.'

Exeter had fetched some of his collection of comics, and Louise recognised Hyperion's costume right away.

'It probably was about sex. Hyperion was a Supervillain, and he certainly did have feelings for your aunt. He used to leave clues to his crimes for the Moon Queen to find just so that she'd follow him, or he'd try and kiss her and get caught that way. He always used to end up in jail.'

'You're not secretly Hyperion, are you?' Louise asked, reaching across the table to touch his fingers. 'You'd better not be.'

Returning to Crystal House, Louise saw Theo hiding among the trees. She called him over. Emboldened by Hyperion's disappearance as a threat, she was going to try something.

'I want to come and visit you in your house today, Theo,' she said. 'Will that be OK?'

Theo looked up at her and nodded.

The sun shone down like an alien thing as Louise followed Theo through the grounds of Crystal House, over the white wall, then across the road and up to his own big wall, where he helped her up and over to the other side.

Once in the grounds of Theo's house, Louise admired the tidy lawns and the healthy trees. She saw the house ahead. Theo did not go to the front door but led her around the side of the house to another lawn.

'You can't come into the house,' he said.

'Why not? You came into mine!'

'I don't think they'll let you in. Can't we just sit on the grass? Wait here. I'll be back in a minute.' Theo ran away and disappeared around a corner.

Alone, Louise looked at the towering clouds above and was reminded of the day she and Exeter had picnicked on this hill and had seen the Chapel of Super Prayer. That chapel had been built through the wall surrounding the grounds of this house. She was on the inside of that wall now.

Then she reflected that, today, she was the one who was being kept out of a house.

Chapter Twenty-Six

Theo certainly was an unusual boy. After Louise had waited on the grass outside his house, he had fetched a model train for her to see and explained that he had been given it on his birthday. Then he had bluntly told her that it was time for her to leave and had led her home again.

Although tonight was stormy, Louise felt secure. There would be no more visits from the strange callers, and she would be leaving here soon anyway.

Later, heavy sheets of rain came down and thunder rolled across the sky. From her bed, in the square of her window, she could see the sick trees blowing in the wind.

Another crash of thunder came. But there had been something different about that sound. Surely it had been far louder than the one before? Then she felt a breeze cross her face and knew that something was terribly wrong. An opening had been made somewhere in the house.

That final crash had not been thunder. It had been the sound of someone breaking in. She heard footsteps on broken glass. She got out of bed and rushed silently to the top of the stairs.

'Theo? Is that you again?'

There was a heavy creak from below, the sound of cautious but heavy footsteps, followed by a long silence. A shadow fell across the wall of the stairwell and stopped. It was still, more like a shadow cast by a piece of furniture than a living being.

'Bale!' a rasping voice said.

Louise nearly died with shock as a huge grey shape stepped up the stairs, like a man, but made from huge, squared-off sheets of metal. The riveted grey body was covered in scorch marks and gouges from past battles. It was the Lead Coffin. On TV, she had seen him club people to death.

She looked up at where she imagined his face to be.

'I'm glad you could come,' she said, in some attempt to keep him calm, to get some kind of control over the situation.

The Lead Coffin stood there for some seconds, then slowly raised his arm. Louise cringed back towards her rooms.

'You're scaring me,' she said. 'Please, just stay there. Stay still. Please, can... can I get you some coffee?'

He ignored her. Then, with a springing groan, his arm swung sideways and slammed into the wall. Dust flew everywhere. But his fist was stuck in the plaster, and that gave Louise time to dart behind him. She raced downstairs towards the front door, looked back, and heard the Coffin reach the top of the stairs.

'Meet death, Bale!' the Coffin hissed as he began to clamber down towards her, lifting his arm again. But then, incredibly, a section of the stairs beneath him tilted, and he was tipped into the wall. He fell with a metallic crash.

When he tried to pick himself up again, Louise saw a long, cobweb-like thread extend itself from the wall and touch him. It was like the cobweb she had seen when the first estate agent had called. There was a spark, an electric flash, and the Lead Coffin roared as smoke began to pour from his casing. The cobweb strand flickered and vanished. The Lead Coffin leaned on a radiator to steady himself, but the bars of the radiator moved apart, letting his hand slip between them, and the gap closed. He was trapped.

'I will destroy you, Bale!'

The Coffin braced himself, and then with a screech of metal that seemed to shake the whole house, he tore the radiator from the wall.

His arm swung the radiator towards Louise, but she dodged aside. The Coffin turned, off-balance, as Louise ran back the other way, into the main part of the house. She ran into the Moon Room, and a flash of lightning shot shadows of the Moon Chair and the writhing branches of the trees across the floor. She stood there, holding onto the chair arm. The Lead Coffin appeared in the doorway, armour still smoking. Louise heard one of the silver women toppling, back in the corridor, crashing to the ground. She didn't know what had happened out there. The Coffin came into the room.

Then a flat panel above the doorway opened to let a thick grey syrup slump down on top of him. Louise saw his metal head begin to dissolve in the viscous, steaming liquid, and then her own eyes began to water from the acrid smell. The Coffin stumbled forward, fell onto his knees, and began screaming. One of his metal hands reached out and wrenched at the arm of the Moon Chair, but it held fast.

The room was full of choking smoke. Louise shut her eyes and cowered by the window. And then the Lead Coffin was upright again, despite all the smoke that rose from his upper body. He advanced again towards her, his arm slamming into the Moon Chair but still unable to move it. Louise was quicker. She scrambled around behind the chair and got back out into the corridor. She ran back through the house, towards the secret exit, but had forgotten the huge sideboard she had moved in front of it.

Chapter Twenty-Seven

The Young Master was awoken by the thunder. He looked around the room and saw AM-8 there, his casing lit by the flickering of the storm. The robot began to move closer to the bed. AM-8 was familiar, yet, in this storm, the Young Master felt himself shy away.

'It is time for you to awake, Sir,' AM-8 said. 'Sir, it is time to awake, time for Silver Control...'

A crash of thunder echoed across the room, and AM-8 said no more.

'I'm already awake!' the Young Master yelled, but now the robot did not respond at all.

The Young Master went out to the corridor. He called for more robots, but none came. Lightning lit the tapestries all around the walls. Then there was just darkness and the sound of rain. The Young Master tried a heavy old light switch, but nothing happened. Normally the robots would work the lights, but now there seemed to be no power at all in the house.

The lightning began to flicker almost continuously. The Young Master was terrified, but then he looked up at the tapestries and was comforted. In the jagged light, the flying Heroes seemed to come alive.

Later, the house lights came back on, and the Young Master saw AM-8 approaching again.

'Have you awakened, Sir?'

'Yes, AM-8, and I'm glad to see you awake again, too.'

'Sir? Where are Silver Control?'

'What?'

'Silver Control, Sir. Are you *sure* you are awake? The house robots cut the power and stood down in order for you to be reawakened by Silver Control, but *are* you reawakened?' AM-8 came up to stand close to him. 'You have not been reawakened, Sir.'

AM-8's head began a frantic clicking.

'You are *not* reawakened, Sir,' the robot repeated at last, 'and there is no response from

Silver Control. There is danger nearby, Sir, and now *you* must command.'

Chapter Twenty-Eight

Louise ran up the back stairs, screaming. Once in her room, she slammed the door shut behind her and leaned on it, listening, but could not hear the Coffin approaching. She waited there for several minutes. Then, from the direction of the main stairs, she heard a thudding and a screech of metal, as if the Coffin had been slowly creeping up but had been caught by yet another trap.

'I will kill you! I will destroy you and your house!' he sounded in terrible pain.

Louise crept out to see what had happened. From the top of the main stairs, she saw the shape of the Coffin below. His arm had become enmeshed in another of the radiators, and one of the stairs he had been standing on had dropped away beneath him again, tipping him sideways into the wall. He had been stupid to get caught the same way a second time. He was trying to wrench the radiator from its mountings but was still trapped, with his leg stuck through the stairs. A motor started up, and then the Coffin began to scream again. Louise saw grinding wheels revolving in the hole in the stairs, cutting into the armour of the Coffin's foot, dragging him further down.

But then he began to use his arms, and with the loudest rending groan, he was free. He straightened himself up against the wall and then resumed climbing the stairs. One of his legs was now bright metal where the grinding wheels had scoured it. Louise did not retreat. She knew now that Crystal House was protecting her.

A steel beam abruptly burst out from the plasterwork at one side, swung into the Lead Coffin, and pinned him against the wall again. Another cobweb-thin wire shot out. There was a flash, and the Coffin gave another terrifying cry. The steel beam released him, and the Coffin fell and lay still. Behind him, water sprays began dousing the flames on the stairs.

Louise ran down the drive in the rain. She ran all the way until she reached the

Peacock Motel. She ran into the lobby. A woman was at the desk, not Exeter. The woman stared at her. Louise realised that she had her bald head exposed, having lost her hairpiece somewhere, and was still in her nightclothes. Then Exeter came.

'What is it? Is it because of Hyperion?'

'What?'

'Hyperion. Didn't you see it on TV? He was killed in a car crash tonight.'

Exeter stood by the main road outside Crystal House to guide in the police cars. The Lead Coffin still lay on the stairs. The policemen hurried into the house. Exeter told them who the Lead Coffin was, but the police just stared at the fallen metal casing as if they had trouble believing their eyes. The Lead Coffin had broken in through a window in one of the side rooms, with strength enough to break even the toughest glass.

Exeter saw that the police had no idea what to do next, so he offered to get the Coffin's head off so they could see if its human driver was still alive inside. Louise wondered if he'd seen how to do it in a comic. Exeter began twisting the blackened metal. The catches of the neck connection scraped reluctantly, but they opened, and then Exeter carefully swivelled the Coffin's helmet right off. A grizzled old face from inside just glanced at him and then looked at Louise with hate.

'You're not even the *real* Moon Queen,' the old face sneered. 'I don't know why I bothered. You're just some tedious, dull, *housewife.*'

As he didn't look too badly hurt, the police and Exeter dragged the man out from his armour in case he managed to reactivate it. Louise saw the bloody exposed bone of his foot where the grinding wheel had cut right through the armour and into him. Police paramedics held the Coffin between them and made him as comfortable as they could before taking him down the stairs.

'He's not in too bad shape. We'll get him outside, ready for the ambulance,' one of them said. But then they stopped at the front door - it had closed, and they found they could not open it. One of them turned the handle, but still the door stayed shut. The Lead Coffin gave a mumble of anger and put out his hand to the door, but then there was a loud crack and a flash of electricity. The Coffin gave a cry as he was jerked rigid by electric shock.

'Door handle - it's live!' one of the policemen yelled, letting him fall. Little flames lapped from Coffin's hand where it had touched the door. He was dead.

'I just touched that door handle myself!' the other cop said.

'There must have been some sort of residual electric charge in his costume,' Exeter said, 'and then when he touched the handle it went to earth.'

When the police and ambulance were gone, Louise and Exeter went to look at the remains of the Lead Coffin's armour. It still lay on the stairs. Exeter said nothing until the sound of the cars had faded away.

'It wasn't static from his costume that killed him,' Exeter said. 'It was Crystal House.'

Chapter Twenty-Nine

Exeter called at Crystal House again the next day. Louise got him to help move the sideboard away from in front of the secret door. He looked nervous today. Then, when she made them each a coffee, he said that he would be going away.

'I'm going down to the Oil Lands to find my sister,' he said. 'It's been too long with no word now, and I want to make sure she's OK. But I don't like leaving you alone here, so please use that room that's free at the Peacock if you ever need to get out of Crystal House.'

'But you can't have a room spare just for me. It's the summer. This must be your busy time.'

'Don't worry about that. It's a room that's been under refurbishment. In fact, I'll send the builders on here afterwards to repair your stairs.'

Louise knew that he was lying about the room and was keeping it free just for her, but she was grateful.

'I'll pay you.'

Then they heard light footsteps and a voice calling out, 'Hello?' Louise could tell it was Theo. He came in and saw Louise, Exeter, and the Lead Coffin's ruined exoskeleton. He went past them to look at it.

'That's what it was,' he said. 'That's what the robots meant when they said they had to awaken me.'

He looked at Louise and Exeter standing together and opened his mouth to speak again, but did not. He just turned and ran away.

'Who was that?' Exeter asked.

'Theo Banks. He's from next door. I went round there one day, but...'

'Theo Banks!' Exeter exclaimed. 'He's not a boy. He's a Superhero like your aunt. He's the *Die Master*.'

'What?'

Exeter began to explain, but Louise couldn't take it in.

'Sorry Exeter, you'll have to tell me another time. My head's going round.'

'OK, Louise. But before I go, there's just one last thing. You know I'm arranging the Summer Festival here at Crescent City and, as usual, it's themed around Superheroes. I was thinking: Would you be willing to take part? Would you be willing to represent your aunt and appear as the Moon Queen? My friend Larry Chill's taking over the organisation of the festival while I'm away.'

'It's still going ahead, even after all that's been happening?'

'We couldn't give it up. We're doing it as a mark of respect for Golden Man and Glinda.'

A week after Exeter left for the South, a special team of police from Steel Ring City arrived to remove the Lead Coffin's armour from Crystal House. These police were brisk and efficient and asked a lot of pushy questions. They wanted to look over the whole house, but Louise wouldn't let them, and when they left she closed the front door firmly behind them. She spent the rest of the day with her thoughts.

The next morning was dull, and Louise got up late. With Exeter gone she was beginning to feel isolated. The weather deteriorated during the day. Leaves from the sick trees blew onto the windows and stuck to them.

Louise knew she should get out of the house, go into the town and mix with humanity, but with Exeter gone, she felt no enthusiasm for anything. She would wait until he came back, she thought. There would be no real need to leave the house until then.

The doorbell rang. *Theo*, she thought, *the 'Die Master'*. She didn't know what to think of him now. But she imagined him outside, waiting in the rain, and she thought that if she did not answer the door soon, he might use the secret entrance. She did not want that opened, in case the recently-departed police might still be watching the house. So she went downstairs, released the locks, and rolled the front door back. It was Jeff who stood on the doorstep.

Chapter Thirty

'Hi, Louise, can we talk?'

Louise was bewildered. Jeff had come in through the front door before she could think about what was happening.

'Listen, Louise,' Jeff said. 'I'm sorry about what happened. Sorry about what I did. I really do apologise. I'll understand if you want to send me away again. But I heard on TV that you'd been attacked by the Lead Coffin, so I had to come and make sure you were OK.'

He was looking at her wig as if he was deciding that the damage he'd done to her was not too bad after all, and was thinking he would be forgiven.

'I really didn't mean what I did. I was just as scared by what happened as you must have been. I don't know why I did it. I've been thinking about it ever since. How can I make it up to you? Can you ever forgive me, Louise?'

'I'll get us some coffee,' she said numbly. 'Wait here. By the door.'

Louise stood in her little kitchen for several seconds before she switched the kettle on, thinking about how, after all her fears of strange callers, she had so casually let Jeff into the house. Then she heard his footsteps. Jeff had not waited by the door.

She tried to calm herself by thinking that perhaps, now that so many other people had come into the house, there was no danger anymore. Perhaps her troubles had worn themselves out. Jeff *had* been her boyfriend after all, and, with Exeter away, she did feel lonely.

'What a place!' Jeff said as he came into the kitchen. 'Those silver women and everything. This is a completely mad house.'

He was leaning in the kitchen doorway, blocking Louise's escape.

'I have come to apologise, Louise. That's all. If you want anything from me, surely that must be what you want - for me to apologise.'

Louise found two cups. But one was the cup Exeter had used. She didn't want Jeff using that, so she put it back on the shelf and took another one.

'So you know Harry Wildwood?' she asked him.

'He's a good bloke. Told me he'd been up here to see you. Said you looked as if you were cracking up a bit.'

Louise handed Jeff his coffee. Then, as he took the cup back into the main part of the house, she followed him.

'This is an amazing place,' Jeff said.

They were in the Moon Room. Jeff went over to the Moon Chair and rested his hand on it.

'Please don't touch that.'

He looked at her as if she was stupid.

'It's just a shock to me that you've called here,' she said. 'Will you leave now and maybe come back tomorrow? Are you staying in Crescent City, or just passing through?'

'I came especially to see *you*, Louise,' Jeff said. 'I can stay in Crescent City for as long as you like. I just wanted to make things right between us again. I know it's not something I can expect right away. I'll go now, but I'll call back at about the same time tomorrow.'

Louise watched Jeff walk away down the drive and remembered the last time she'd seen him. He had completely destroyed her that day.

Chapter Thirty-One

Exeter left the aeroplane and hurried across the tarmac to the queue by the shed. There was just a short line of civilians there, on various errands in the war zone, waiting to be warned of the dangers here and to have their passes checked.

'What's your reason for visiting the Oil Lands, Mr. Van Hoyland?' the official asked in English. Exeter explained why he had come, but the official looked at him as if he was just placing an extra burden on the armed forces.

'We can't guarantee your safety, Mr. Van Hoyland. There's a flight leaving soon that will take you home if you want to go back.'

'My sister needs me.'

The official looked sceptical but switched his gaze to the person next in line. Exeter took it that he could go on.

On the bus from the airport, the oven-like heat of the Oil Lands and the people all speaking a language he didn't understand made the threat of danger here seem overpowering. Exeter occupied his mind by thinking about a new decorative scheme he'd had in mind for the Peacock Motel. He felt like doing some more design work or some painting now. He retreated to those thoughts.

The bus passed through poor-looking streets filled with people, possibly refugees. The whole city was filthy. The bus paused, and Exeter looked into a bar. It was full, but no one was drinking. Nearby was a big superstore. It looked alien, but he recognised the name. Soon afterwards the bus stopped in a big square. This reminded him of a dream he'd had once, where he'd been going to work but had been travelling with a wrong ticket. Thoughts of the dream and the Peacock Motel stayed until he made a decision and stood up, pushing back among the people who were boarding the bus. He got off and walked back to the superstore he'd seen.

Inside, the store was the same as back home, except that they could not control the heat, and some of the brands were unfamiliar. At first, he thought there was no selection of art supplies, but then he saw them, right on the back wall.

A television was playing nearby. He ignored it because he did not want to hear any more news about the war. He looked at the racks of oil paints, the familiar colours soothing him as if they were old friends. He saw a stack of new canvases and thought he might buy a couple of small ones and some tubes of paint. But the canvases were all too big.

He flicked through a rack of posters, and then he saw it - a poster of the presidential building down here in the South. The president of the Oil Lands stood on the balcony, waving at a crowd, and behind him stood Morthwil.

Exeter felt his stomach clench. The heat and the smell of the shop was getting to him. He looked at the poster again and then noticed that it wasn't just Morthwil who stood behind the president on that balcony. Morthwil's face also belonged to someone else.

He forgot all about finding his sister. He had to get back to Crescent City, to Louise, and warn her at once.

Chapter Thirty-Two

The next day, Louise let Jeff into Crystal House again.

'So who have you met since you came to live here?' Jeff asked. 'Who are your friends?'

Louise told him about Exeter and about Theo. She didn't mention who Theo truly was.

'So you know a man from a restaurant and the kid from next door. What a social whirl!' Jeff laughed. They were walking through the house, and Louise saw Jeff's and her own reflections twisted together as they passed in front of one of the silver women. She showed him the place on the stairs where the Lead Coffin had been caught by the house. Jeff looked at her as if she was joking. Then Louise suddenly thought that Jeff might be thinking she was taking him up the stairs for another reason, so she turned and hurried back down. Disorientated, she led him back through the house until they came to the back stairs.

'What's here?' Jeff asked, and then Louise found that she was telling him all about the secret exit.

'Where?' said Jeff, not believing her, because the door was so well disguised. He stood by the window, running his hands all along the wall. 'A joke, right, Louise? There's nothing here.'

He came to the place, touched it, and the whole secret door with its section of window swung smoothly aside like a dream.

'Don't you keep it locked?' he said after a few seconds.

'There is no lock,' Louise said. 'It's a secret way out. It doesn't have to be locked. That would just slow me down.'

'Who else knows about this, Louise?'

'Theo, the boy from next door. He showed it to me. He knew my aunt...'

'Never mind that. You need to get a proper lock for this, Louise. You've got to be safe. Come on, tell me. Who else knows about this? You don't even *know*, do you? You can't have an open door in your house. I'll get a lock fitted. Is there any furniture, anything we can place in front of it for now?'

'Don't worry, Jeff, I'm OK with it.'

'Don't be *stupid*, Louise. You don't know how many people know about that way in. You've had the Lead Coffin busting in here.'

'He didn't come in that way.'

'You've been attacked. Far worse than anything I did. You've got to seal up that door. Fit a lock. You have to make sure you stay safe.'

Jeff came closer to her. She backed away.

'Listen to me, Louise, I want you to fix that door shut!'

She shuddered.

'You'll let me fit a lock?' Jeff placed his hand on her shoulder.

Jeff came back from Crescent City with some fat white window locks and a power drill to install them, and then set to work. He took the new drill from its packaging. When he saw Louise watching him, he whirred the bit playfully in the direction of her face. Louise hated what Jeff was doing but half-believed now that he was probably right. It must be sensible for the door to have a lock. After all, how much difference could it make in the time taken to escape if she just had to undo a couple of locks?

What Jeff did to the secret door was very ugly. The new locks revealed its previously hidden shape.

'OK?'

Louise nodded reluctantly. Then Jeff took hold of her, gripping her arms hard. He took it for granted that she would not mind if he kissed her. As he pushed his lips into her face, Louise looked over his shoulder at the new locks, at this disfigurement of Crystal House. Jeff had already ruined her once, and now he was doing it again.

'Get away from me!'

'Wha...?'

'Get AWAY!'

Jeff gave a brittle little smile, but he did leave the house. Outside, he stood there, looking at the diseased trees, until he noticed a pair of eyes staring at him.

'Who's there? Come on out!'

Theo stepped out from the undergrowth.

'Who are you?'

'I'm Theo Banks.'

'Ah, the kid from next door. Well, I don't think it's a good idea for you to come here, Theo. This is private property, and you can't just come in and start wandering around here whenever you please.'

'Miss Bale said...'

'Well, I'm Miss Bale's boyfriend, and I'm telling you...'

'You're not her boyfriend.'

'That's enough. Now get lost or I'll give you a smack!'

'Only Miss Bale can tell me when to go.'

Anger flashed into Jeff's face. He pushed Theo back against one of the pulpy trees and slapped him across the face.

'I told you, kid: *Get Lost.*'

Tears of rage came to Theo's eyes as he stumbled away. For a short time, unnoticed in Crystal House, the silver women's eyes blazed red.

Exeter hurried from the store, everything forgotten except that he had to warn Louise about what he'd just seen. She had to get away from Crystal House.

A roar deafened him as planes zoomed overhead, their markings confirming that he was truly in a foreign land. What could he do? How could he get a message back home? He went up to an old man and asked him about telephones, but the old man just looked at him with pity and said that nothing worked in this town.

Chapter Thirty-Three

The Young Master was walking past the Library when U-3 stepped from the shadows. Then AM-12 appeared in the Library door.

'How much do you remember, Sir?' AM-12 said.

'I have no memories, AM-12. Why do you ask?'

'Have you recently been to the Wall?'

'The Wall? I don't know what that is,' the Young Master said, as if he had never even heard the word before. AM-12 and U-3 stood regarding him for a few seconds, then walked away together.

'Listen, Jeff,' Louise said. 'I'm not sure about those locks after all. Can't we take them off? What if Theo comes here and he can't get in?'

'You don't want kids just coming in here whenever they want. We could be in bed or something...' Jeff was thinking too far ahead, but Louise didn't seem to have been listening to him.

'Theo's my friend,' Louise said, missing Jeff's grin as he noticed he'd got away with his remark. 'I like to see him. If it wasn't for Theo I wouldn't even know about that secret door. He's showed me a lot of other things as well. And he's not just a child. Exeter told me...'

'That's enough. Shut up now, Louise.'

'No, wait, Jeff. Theo's not just a child. He showed me some of the other defences of the house.'

'Well, OK, Louise, so now you can show them to me.'

Louise would have preferred it if Jeff had gone away, but she found herself standing next to the chrome console table in the Moon Room. She moved the hidden lever and told Jeff to look out of the window as the Moon Queen dummy thumped up from out of the ground outside. The dummy's cape moved slightly in the breeze. Then Louise pushed the lever back the other way and the dummy dropped back again.

'Bring it up again,' Jeff said. 'I'm going outside to take a look.'

Louise watched through the window as Jeff went up to the Moon Queen dummy. He stood in front of it, staring at the mask, where the face would be, then looked back at Louise. She saw his lecherous look even from this far away. Then she remembered herself wearing a similar mask and hoped she would have the strength to avoid ever telling Jeff about that. Jeff put his hands onto the dummy, touching its face, then he moved his hands down to feel its breasts, then down again until he found that the dummy was incomplete below the waist, the emptiness there hidden by its swirling cape. The top half of the body was supported by a metal bar.

'Listen,' Jeff yelled back to Louise, 'I've got some things to take care of. I'll be back tomorrow, OK?'

Exeter just about managed to catch sight of a packed city bus as it drove away. He stopped, discouraged and sweating, and looked at the hundreds of people in the square. Finally, another bus came. An old woman, who must have seen the worry in his face, told Exeter to go in front of her in the queue.

The hospital where his sister worked was at the end of this bus route, but something was wrong. The rest of the passengers had all got off at the previous stop. He was the only one left for the hospital stop. The driver said something in the local language that Exeter didn't understand, but then he saw what the driver had meant - the hospital had been abandoned. The driver said something else, but Exeter shook his head and got off the bus.

Chapter Thirty-Four

Outside the windows of Crystal House, the diseased trees blew back and forth as sheets of rain sloughed across the garden. The thick clouds made it dark, almost like night, and leaves fluttered down from the unhealthy trees. Blown-down branches covered the ground, as if this house no longer had any part to play in the world except to gradually fade away and die. A lot of debris had fallen from those trees last night. It was the night when Louise had finally given in.

A gust of wind blew a rattle of raindrops into the window right in front of where she stood, as she felt again the fateful knowledge that Jeff was now completely back in her life. He came through from the bedroom and stood behind her, completely naked, in the doorway.

She remembered what he had said in bed that morning - *I knew you'd have me back. We belong together, you and me.'*

Exeter walked away from the abandoned hospital. He'd found no clue to what had happened there. He went back the way the bus had come. He had thought of waiting for the next bus, but hanging around would have been too dispiriting. He had to do something, even if it meant using up all the energy and enthusiasm he had left.

He tried to think of fun things to cheer himself up. He remembered giving Louise that Moon Queen costume. But that reminded him of the danger she was still in. After an hour he reached the chain store with the poster again. He could go in and buy it now, just to finally confirm that what he had seen was true. He went towards the entrance, but now the shutters were down. The store was shut.

Louise was cooking while Jeff sat in the living room. Thankfully, he'd been quiet for a long while, but then she heard his voice call through.

'You didn't tell me you had this!' His voice came from the bedroom now. Louise had not expected him to start looking around in there. She ran to him and found him holding the Moon Queen costume.

'Put that back, Jeff.'

He grinned.

'Does it fit you? Did you find it in the house?'

'No, Exeter gave it to me.'

'Exeter? Your friend from the hotel?'

'He's been a good friend to me since I came here.'

'*How* good a friend, Louise?'

'He's looked after me, ever since I came here. I think he's gay. He's never tried anything. He's been really good. I told you, his motel is called the Peacock. He said I could always go there. He even keeps a room for me in case I get scared.'

'He's set up a little *love nest*, you mean?'

'No. Nothing like that. I go there to eat, most days, and we talk...'

'You *eat* with him?'

Louise tried to smile.

'There's nothing going on, Jeff,' she said, 'I'm sure he's gay, and he's not even in Crescent City at the moment. He's gone to the South to find his sister.'

'What have you been getting up to, Louise?' Jeff grabbed her wrists and forced her back against the wall.

In the morning, Exeter awoke uncomfortably on the ground in a small park, his mind full of confusion and worry. He thought again of the poster. If what he had seen was true, then the danger threatening Louise was worse than anything the Lead Coffin had ever done.

Chapter Thirty-Five

'A very slick place,' Jeff said, as he stopped his car outside the Peacock Motel. He got out and went around to Louise's side, to prevent her from opening the door until he had run his eyes all over the building. Then the friendly peacock bobbed into view. 'And here's the peacock,' he added mirthlessly. 'Come on.'

He opened Louise's door.

A man Louise had never met before had watched them arrive and came to greet them, smiling. He looked just as friendly as Exeter did.

'Hello,' he said. 'You must be Louise Bale. I'm Exeter's friend, Larry Chill.'

Jeff spoke first.

'Show us this room your pal keeps here for Louise.'

Larry Chill led them through to the residential part of the motel. He tried to make conversation, saying he'd not heard from

Exeter yet. Louise wanted to reply, but when she opened her mouth Jeff gripped her arm painfully hard.

They arrived at the room kept for Louise. Inside it smelled of paint and was so clean that it was obvious that the place was completely unused, but Jeff still looked at Louise suspiciously. Chill, friendly as ever, suggested that they join him later in the restaurant for a drink.

'We'll come now, Mr. Chill,' Jeff said.

Then, on the way to the restaurant, they passed through the piano lounge with Moon Queen memorabilia adorning its walls.

'What's all this stuff in here?' Jeff said.

'Oh, that's part of Exeter's Moon Queen collection,' Chill replied. 'He loves all the Superhero things, and anything about the Moon Queen in particular. I must say that he and I are both especially pleased that Miss Bale has agreed to appear in this summer's Crescent City Festival.'

Louise had not yet mentioned that to Jeff. He nodded, unsmiling, and gripped her arm again.

'Exeter has more items than this,' Chill said, obliviously. 'Most of his collection is in his private apartment.'

'May we see that, please?' Jeff said.

'Well, it is Exeter's private apartment.' Chill looked surprised.

'Your pal gave instructions that Louise could come to this motel whenever she liked, didn't he?' Jeff said. 'I'm sure he wouldn't mind if she went in there.'

Chill nodded doubtfully and then led Jeff and Louise down to Exeter's basement flat. Louise had never been here before and, as Chill unlocked the door, felt as if they were completely abusing Exeter's hospitality.

'You can go now,' Jeff said. Chill looked at him in surprise but went back upstairs.

Jeff waited until Chill had gone before going into Exeter's room. It was decorated just like the main part of the hotel. The walls were the same colours, and the same kind of display cases stood around. But there were a series of filing cabinets that were labelled as housing his comics collection. Jeff tugged at the handle of one of them.

'Don't do this, Jeff. There's nothing to see.'

They found no key to the filing cabinets, but Jeff burst one of them open. Louise saw the files of comics inside. Jeff took some of them out and began to leaf through. They were Moon Queen comics. Then he noticed a larger box, like a plan chest. He had more difficulty opening that, but then when he did get it open an unpleasant look of satisfaction came into his eyes. Louise didn't know what to think, whether it would be good or bad for her that Jeff had found something he liked.

'Look at *these*, Louise!' Jeff said, lifting up a large sheet of paper.

It was a far more elaborate drawing than the usual comic artwork, and it showed the Moon Queen stretched out provocatively, semi-naked, on a tiger-print rug.

'Still think your friend's so innocent? *Gay?*' Jeff snapped as he pulled out picture after picture. They were all in the same style, all showing the Moon Queen in bizarre erotic poses. 'What do you think of your friend now?'

The airport now reminded Exeter of the hospital. Security gates were shut across the entrance. Exeter asked a soldier if there was any way he could get a flight home, to the North, but when he spoke, the soldier just shook his head and pretended not to understand.

Exeter stepped back in frustration, then threw himself back on the gates in fury, shouting, and gripped onto the wire mesh, twisting into it with his fingers. The soldier just looked at him. Exeter realised he had been lucky. He would be of no help to Louise or to his sister if he got shot. Someone in the crowd laughed as he let go of the mesh and went away again.

Chapter Thirty-Six

Back at Crystal House, Jeff sat on the bed, holding Louise's Moon Queen costume and rubbing into the material with his thumbs.

'Just a 'good friend', and he gives you *this*? And now he wants you to appear, wearing it, in public, while all the time he has those dirty pictures. You know what? Your friend's a pervert. What's been happening between you and your pervert, Louise? What have you got mixed up in?'

'But he has everything *else,* too - all of the Superhero stuff. He's a collector, Jeff. If he saw those posters about her he'd buy them, wouldn't he? He'd collect anything at all to do with the Moon Queen.'

'It sounds like he's collected *you.* Have you ever worn this costume in front of him?'

'Of course not.'

'So you say. OK, just put the mask on for me then. Let's see what it looks like.'

Louise took the mask, then hesitantly raised it to her head. Jeff looked away as she removed her wig. But then he began watching her again as, standing in front of the mirror, she began to smooth the Moon Queen mask down over the upper part of her face. He came up behind her, took her by the shoulders, and spun her around.

'I think you'll look good in *all* of it.'

'No.'

'You'll put the whole costume on,' Jeff said in a voice that Louise knew she had better obey. Jeff sat down on the bed again and moistened his lips as Louise began to remove her clothes. She stepped hurriedly into the legs of the body stocking and pulled it up, adjusting it around her shoulders. Then she clipped on the cape. Finally, she stood in front of him.

'You were lying to me, Louise. You knew exactly how to put that on. Tell me now what you've been getting up to!'

'I haven't done anything...'

Jeff lunged for her, but Louise was too quick. She sped from the room, out into the main part of the house. There was no time to escape through the secret door - Jeff had seen to that. She ran down the main stairs.

'LOUISE?' Jeff's voice echoed through the house. Even the Lead Coffin had not been as frightening as Jeff was now. Louise reached the front door and struggled to unlock it, to run back the bolts, but they wouldn't move. She whispered hoarsely to the house that it wasn't being fair. Jeff appeared at the top of the stairs.

'Stay there. I'm coming down.'

He reached the place on the stairs where the Lead Coffin had been trapped by the house's defences, but nothing happened. He kept on coming down.

Louise ran back through the house, past the Moon Room and the silver women. She reached the secret door and grabbed the keys to the new locks from their hook, but she knew she wouldn't have time to open them. Jeff's footsteps came from the corridor behind her. She began to climb the back stairs.

'Save me!' she called out to the house, but still nothing happened. Jeff followed her, closer all the time. He ran up the last few steps and grabbed her by the cape.

Louise felt the cape pulling up against the side of her face. She kicked out and felt her toes stub as they hit Jeff's leg. He stepped back with a cry of surprise and let go. Louise saw the scowl on his face that she remembered. She ran along the top corridor and back down the front stairs. She looked up at one of the giant silver women and saw her terrified reflection looking back.

Jeff was coming down the main stairs again. This time, as he reached the bottom, he spread his arms wide, blocking Louise's way. She stumbled and backed into what she had always thought was a blind alcove, but now she found that it was a long, radiator-lined corridor with the Moon Room at its end, as if the house had changed its shape. But there was no time to think of that. She turned, feeling her cape streaming behind her as she ran. She heard Jeff's running footsteps.

There was a loud buzzing sound from the radiators, followed by a whimper and a thud from just behind her. She turned around and saw Jeff spill slowly onto the floor, a look of confusion on his face. Then, for a moment, the thought came to Louise that she had left the stove on upstairs - there was a faint smell of cooked meat.

Jeff lay on the floor.

'I can't move my legs. I can't *feel* my legs!' he cried.

He looked around, then pointed at one of the walls.

'Those aren't radiators,' he whispered. 'They must be microwave coils or something.'

'Your legs are bleeding.'

As Louise helped Jeff to his feet, he dug his fingers into her arms as hard as he could, deliberately trying to cause her pain. But she moved him through to the Moon Room. She held onto him until they reached the Moon Chair. There was no other furniture in this part of the house, and so she would have to sit him down there. She lowered him into the chair as gently as she could.

A big man with crutches who had got on a couple of stops back began to work his way up the aisle of the bus. Exeter felt too tired to move but reluctantly offered him his seat. The man sat down gratefully. As the number of people on board thinned out later in the journey, Exeter got another seat, but then he saw that the man with the crutches was trying to get his attention.

'Aero-port closed,' the man said. 'I see you there yesterday. You yell at gate. But I know way...' He winked. Exeter was so tired that he just shook his head in despair. The bus came to the city centre square, and Exeter got off.

The airport was still closed because of the emergency, someone told him, and that was all they knew. But overhead he could hear the drone of a large transport plane from the North.

He got something to drink in a grim basement shop nearby. He knew his only chance had been to talk to the crippled man. But what he *could* do, he thought, was get on another bus and try to find him again.

The bus arrived, not too full this time. Exeter looked around inside, but the man with the crutches was not there. So he sat as near as he could to where he'd sat before. He stayed on the bus until the end of the route, where everyone else got off.

'End,' the driver called to him. 'I go the other way now.' Exeter went to pay his fare back along the route, but the driver took pity on him and told him just to stay on. The bus went back through the streets of the town again, past the still-closed airport, right back to the hospital, but there was still no sign of the man. Again, Exeter went to the driver to pay. This time the driver nodded and took the money.

Chapter Thirty-Seven

Ignoring Jeff's shouts of pain from the Moon Chair, Louise went up to the kitchen and found a big knife. Then she went to the secret door and removed all the window locks. The scars still showed on the wall, but at least the door would open now. She went and looked in at Jeff again. His legs looked very bad.

'I'm going to get you an ambulance,' she said, 'but I don't have a phone here, so I'm going down to the Peacock Motel.'

Jeff began to shudder as if the pain in his legs was terrible. He grabbed her hand and pulled her towards him. She tried to pull back, but Jeff was too strong.

'You're going to get it, Louise. I'm going to...'

There came a high-pitched whining from the chair, like a dentist's drill, and Jeff moaned in fear. He released Louise's hand and sank quickly back into the seat cushion, as if he was being sucked down into it. He began screaming. Louise pulled at Jeff's shoulders to try and drag him off the chair, but then, as Jeff fell forward, she saw a set of horrible, bloody little grinding wheels whirling inside the seat cushion where he had been sitting. What had the chair done to him? Her stomach heaved.

Somehow she managed to drag Jeff upstairs and onto the bed. She turned him over, examined his rear and legs, and bandaged him up with strips of material ripped from a pillowcase.

And then Louise found that she was grinning. Grinning out from the face-mask of the Moon Queen, because, once more, the house had protected her. Something else occurred to her, and she began to laugh out loud - Jeff had made it into her bed yet again, but this time not in the way he'd intended. He was completely defeated.

'I'm going to get you that ambulance now, Jeff,' she said.

'I'm going to say *you* did this to me. You know, Louise, I'm *glad* I burned you that time.'

'Then stay there and bleed, Jeff.'

Louise just went to look at the Moon Chair again. It now looked perfectly clean again, as if nothing had happened there.

The doorbell rang. Louise went to answer it. A taxi man was there, the car behind him with the engine already running.

'Taxi for Miss Bale. To the Superhero Festival,' he said, 'courtesy of Mr. Chill.'

The bus traversed its route again, and Exeter examined every passenger who got on, but none of them was the man with the crutches. He felt himself sinking into a half-sleep, and he looked dazedly out of the window at the lights of the traffic. The bus was approaching the depressing hulk of the hospital again.

He went to pay another fare.

'I make only one more run,' the driver said. 'You buy ticket to aero-port and get off there. It's best for you. In case you get a plane.'

Exeter got off the bus at the airport gate, but it was still shut, and now the immediate area was deserted apart from two sentries standing under a light. So Exeter started walking to the next bus stop. He approached the street where he had visited the chain store. The shutters were down over most of the windows, but a group of men was gathered at the far end. One shutter had been left up, and a TV was playing in the window so that people could still see the news. Exeter looked at the unfamiliar newsreader. One of the men watching looked at him and, for some reason, grinned.

The man said a word Exeter recognised as the name of another town and then tapped his wrist. Exeter showed the man the time. The man started talking fast.

'Bus. Next street. Run. You must run now!'

Could this be a way out of this place that he hadn't known about?

Exeter ran. Around the corner he saw the bus, waiting by the far side of the road. But then he saw a sight he had not expected to see - a phone box with the light on. Did the light mean that the phone itself was operational? The bus engine began to pick up, as if it was about to move off. Exeter would have to run for it now. But the phone box - if he could get a message out - warn Louise - that was the most important thing. He went into the phone box as the bus pulled out. He shoved the card into the slot and dialled the number, but then he knew he'd made the wrong move. There was no tone. The phone was completely dead.

Chapter Thirty-Eight

As Louise came down the steps into the main festival hall in her Moon Queen costume, she was met by a hubbub of noise and conversation. She had planned first of all to find Larry Chill, but now people were turning to stare at her. She had thought she would feel self-conscious, but now she knew that the Moon Queen mask made her scarred head look beautiful. Someone nearby asked if he could take her picture, and she nodded and graciously smiled into the lens.

All around the hall were stalls piled with boxes of comics. There were life-sized cardboard cut-outs of Superheroes, many of whom now looked familiar. She saw some banners advertising Henry's Victual Store as sponsor. Henry had taken the opportunity to come up with a slogan - *Henry's VIIIth! 8% Off Normal Prices During the Superhero Festival,* followed by a picture of a crown. Louise remembered when she had encountered Henry's son, Joe, when he had falsely accused her of shoplifting, and then how one day Joe and his little brother Carl had caused trouble at the Peacock Motel.

A woman at one of the stalls came out from behind her table, smiling and holding up a comic of the Moon Queen.

'Will you sign it?' she asked. 'It's just for me. And may I take your picture?'

Louise nodded. The woman stood next to her, and while Louise signed the comic, a man photographed them. Louise managed another smile. A tiny dog appeared.

'Oh, and one with Butch?' the woman asked. Louise nodded again, although her smile was beginning to feel weak. She was starting to feel like just an exhibit, but she managed to grin at the friendly little dog. Then Larry Chill saw her, came over, and led her towards the conference room.

Louise heard raised voices from behind them. She turned and saw a big old man make his entrance, surrounded by a crowd of admiring people. He had powerfully styled hair and wore a suit with a high yellow collar and a cape attached. It was T-Man, Conway Johns. As Johns and his admirers passed the table where the woman had taken Louise's photo, the little dog, Butch, ran out, barking.

'Please call your dog away,' Johns said coldly. 'He annoys me.'

The woman from the stall scooped the little dog up into her arms.

Larry Chill led Louise to the stage in the conference room, where a big crowd was already waiting. He took her onto the stage, where there was a row of chairs with a long table with microphones, showed her where to sit, and then went away to talk to someone else. Anxious not to have to look at the crowd, Louise examined the place card with her name on it, and then at the one for the next chair along. Conway Johns would be sitting there.

There was a flurry of activity from by the door, and then Johns himself entered the room. He looked up at the stage, saw Louise, and briefly seemed surprised. Louise saw that he must have momentarily thought that she was her aunt before he'd realised that was impossible. He made his way onto the stage and sat down.

Two more of the old Superheroes who Louise did not yet recognise joined them, and then Larry Chill returned and took his place at the end of the table. Curtains began to shut across the windows, and a video began to play on a screen on the wall behind them. Louise turned around and saw a city at night, with mysterious glimmering windows. Next, a closer view, where the city did not look quite so inviting. Then a cut right down to street-level, where three muggers attacked a woman. A younger T-Man, playing himself, swooped down from the sky. When he had defeated the criminals, the music faded, and the video stopped.

The real T-Man stood up and began to speak, his voice echoing around the hall.

'Welcome to Crescent City!' he boomed. 'Welcome to the Crescent City Superhero Festival!'

Louise looked up at his big solid body. Despite his age, he was tremendous and clearly possessed immense power. She wondered how anyone could ever think they could fight him.

'Welcome, friends!' The screen showed glittering laser rainbows. 'Welcome,' T-Man said, a third time. 'The order of events is as follows...'

As T-Man spoke, Louise stifled a laugh at the incongruity of it. When he had first stood up, he had been like a god, and now here he was, talking about where the toilets were.

When Johns had finished speaking, Larry Chill thanked him, and said, 'This festival is dedicated to the memory of the Golden Man and Glinda.

'As you all know, Glinda... vanished recently, and the Golden Man was killed. It's thought that they fought and were defeated by Morthwil. But in honour of them, we continue the festival.'

A muffled cheer and faint clapping came as the audience took hold of the idea.

Then, as Chill began to introduce the first panel discussion, T-Man turned to Louise.

'I saw you smile,' he said. 'When I was speaking, when I described the rooms and gave the order of events, why did you smile?'

'The first item is our 'Getting-To-Know-You' question and answer session,' Larry Chill said. 'On the panel with me, we have Louise Bale, niece of that well-loved Superhero the Moon Queen. Louise Bale, Ladies and Gentlemen. And, direct from Steel Ring City, Conway Johns - *T-Man*!'

Johns stood up to thunderous applause.

'I don't expect Conway will be able to give us any details,' Chill said, 'but I'm sure he's hard at work protecting us and finding out, and avenging, what happened to the Golden Man and Glinda.

'And we have the Tribune, and Captain Z!' More clapping and cheers came as the two other Superheroes stood up and bowed.

When the applause had died down, the first question from the audience was for Conway Johns. It was about a battle years ago that Louise had never heard of. When Johns replied, at first Louise thought he was modestly trying to minimise his involvement, but then, as he continued to speak at length, she saw that it was false modesty. What Johns wanted to do was to ensure that every detail of what had happened was understood and remembered by all, as if he was carefully delineating his autobiography.

Then a question came for Louise about one of her aunt's old adventures. She had to apologise for not knowing the answer.

Thirdly, there was another question for T-Man. The voice of the questioner sounded familiar. Louise looked into the audience and saw that it was Henry's son, Joe.

'Conway Johns?' Joe said. 'Can you tell us something about your early days as a Superhero? Can you tell us how it all began for you?'

Johns opened his mouth to speak as if he had a reply prepared, but then Joe went on.

'What I'd particularly like to know is: I heard that when you first began your career as T-Man, something happened that meant you lost part of your body every time you used your superpowers. How come you're not just some shrivelled-up little guy now?'

There was a trickle of laughter from around the audience. Johns' eyes flicked quickly around at the room and just said, 'That problem was overcome.'

'Conway Johns,' Joe spoke up again. 'Is it true you were once known as *Cup-of-Tea Man?*'

He sniggered and looked at young Carl next to him, who was grinning too.

Johns stood up.

'Despite the fact that your question is impertinent, I will reply,' he said in a low voice. 'The name you have used was indeed coined when, on a rescue, I arrived too late and there were... fatalities.' His voice dropped still further. 'But those deaths were not my responsibility.'

'Than you, Conway,' Larry Chill said, his voice going out clearly across the now silent hall. 'Thank you for that. But now I suggest...'

Carl raised his hand.

'We know that T-Man and the Moon Queen sometimes worked on cases together,' he asked. 'But isn't it true that at some time you were *closer* than just colleagues? Didn't you fancy her? Wasn't there any...'

Larry Chill looked at Johns while Johns stared at Carl as if marking the boy out as an enemy.

Then, very clearly, Johns said, 'You speak, I imagine, of rumours of *romance* between myself and my colleague. Nothing of that kind ever was the case in reality or in fiction. I did not love Agnes Bale.'

Exeter caught the new bus the next morning. It travelled out beyond the city, and so he was now able to see far more of the Oil Lands. He could see now how valuable this place would be to President Rayonier - rows of oil wells stretched across the horizon in front of him. He'd thought he had been here long enough to begin to understand this place, yet he had known nothing.

The bus stopped at a sun shelter where a lot of local people got off, and then, much emptier now, turned off the made-up road onto a much rougher one. The bus bumped across the potholes and eventually approached a set of brown buildings, but before it got there it was flagged down by a man selling radios. The silver plastic of the radios gleamed in the sun. The salesman climbed on board, smiled down the aisle of the bus, and held one up for everyone to see.

More people got on at the brown buildings. Then the bus began to climb a steep hill, and Exeter saw spurts of steam begin to wisp from the radiator cap.

Chapter Thirty-Nine

When the panel broke for lunch, Conway Johns followed Louise to the canteen and sat right next to her there.

'I did *not* have any kind of romantic relationship with your aunt,' he repeated.

'Everyone in the world seems to have been crazy about my aunt,' Louise said. 'I'm surprised you weren't. And you built all those defences for Crystal House. Why did you do that if you didn't love her too?'

'There was no love affair between myself and the Moon Queen,' Conway Johns said. 'That was not the case.'

Louise looked at him, irked by his behaviour. Why was he denying something that was so obviously true?

'Wait a minute, I'm sure I remember my aunt once saying something about you.'

'She spoke of me? What did she say?' There was an intense interest in Johns' face now. Louise wondered whether she dared go on.

'She told me that you were very dull, and that she was actually in love with Hyperion. That's what she said.' Louise smiled right into Johns' face as blatantly as she could, but then her mouth fell open. She was unprepared for the rage she saw in Johns' eyes.

'Hyperion was the most disgusting creature ever to have crawled on the face of this earth!'

Then T-Man stood up, catching the table with his hip. The table rolled over onto its side, and the plates hit the floor with a crash.

'Hyperion died as easily as the Golden Man and his absurd wife!' T-Man yelled.

'What about when my boyfriend Jeff Butler came to see you?' Louise asked. 'What happened then? Why wouldn't you see him when he called at your house? I had to suffer for that! I bet you're *really* good, though,' she went on. 'I expect you're really brave. I expect you always win just because everyone else is always weaker than you are.'

Johns was standing in front of her now, and Louise felt as if his eyes were boring into her.

'Best not to speak of matters of which you know nothing!' Johns said. He strode away through the stunned and silent canteen.

Back on stage that afternoon, Louise stole the Tribune's chair to avoid sitting next to T-Man again. The Tribune and Captain Z saw that she'd moved and grinned at her as they came in. But then Louise felt a form lower itself into Captain Z's chair. T-Man was not going to let her escape that easily. She felt his huge side leaning into her. Then Larry Chill arrived and nodded encouragingly at her as he took his place and turned to face the audience.

'This afternoon we discuss the fact and fiction of the Superheroes in the comics,' he announced. Images began to flicker onto the screen on the wall, comics that Louise now recognised, while Chill gave a short speech about the various artists and writers who had delineated the Superheroes' adventures. As Chill went on to discuss the Superhero comic strips, Louise's attention wandered until she saw that the screen was showing a drawing of her aunt, posing half-naked. Conway Johns began to breathe heavily. Louise remembered the erotic Moon Queen posters in Exeter's collection and now saw how that kind of art fitted into the world of comics that surrounded the Superheroes. Conway Johns' lungs breathed in great volumes of air.

Then, unexpectedly, a fly landed on the table in front of her, and she was reminded of Hyperion again. She remembered the flies she had seen when he had been in Crystal House. Johns leaned forward and put his thumb down and crushed the fly flat.

Larry Chill was still showing pictures of Superheroes up on the screen. A drawing of Morthwil came up, and Louise felt the muscles tighten in T-Man's side again. Then he suddenly twisted in his chair and looked down at her.

What Louise saw was unbelievable. She saw that the face staring down into hers was the same as the face on the screen - Conway Johns was Morthwil. Morthwil was Conway Johns. They were identical. They were the same person.

Exeter walked disconsolately through a crowd of tents, trying to get away from the milling people just for a moment so that he could think. Eventually, he came to a patch of rocky ground and sat among the boulders. He caught sight of his suit and saw how filthy it was. And then he saw something incredible - a jeep drove by, and driving it was a nurse. It wasn't his sister, but it meant that hospital staff might be close.

Chapter Forty

Later, when someone else from the audience raised his hand to ask him a question, Conway Johns just stared out from the stage as if he hadn't heard anything. He just sat there until the questioner put his hand down again. Then Carl, still sitting in the audience, called out.

'Who was the strongest Superhero?'

Chill smiled with relief, glad to hear what he thought would be a non-contentious question. 'T-Man' was so obviously the correct answer.

'We all know how T-Man is the most powerful,' Chill said, hoping to answer for Johns, who was still staring blankly ahead of him. 'Only he could have fought Morthwil and defeated him in their famous battle in the stratosphere.'

But then Johns stood up. He looked at Chill, at Louise, then at Carl, and then around the room.

'You expect me to boast of my powers,' he said. 'Yet I am not powerful. I am weak.'

Louise wondered what Johns was going to say. Was he going to admit that he was also Morthwil?

'Paradoxically, the source of my weakness is also my strength,' T-Man said. 'I have the powers you know of, and also more powers of which humanity has not yet dreamed.'

He looked at Louise.

'I find it very easy to *despise* you people,' he said. 'You self-absorbed little creatures, who run around full of your self-importance, constantly needing to be rescued from your stupidity. It is hard to do good. It is such a struggle to maintain my... love for you, you who are so undeserving.'

He turned back to face the room.

'Please understand me. This is not reality. These thoughts come to me in my loneliness. I have no equal. There is no-one, on the earth, of my stature, and I have been forced to dwell for too long among you.'

Louise was shocked to see a tear trickle from the corner of Johns' eye. He stopped speaking and just stood there, looking out over the room.

'An interesting insight into your philosophy, Conway,' Larry Chill said blandly, before asking a question of Captain Z and the Tribune. Conway Johns, seemingly now lost in a world of his own, slowly sat down again.

Louise stood up.

'Toilet,' she whispered to Larry Chill so that T-Man would not guess that she was running away. Behind her, she heard Joe's voice again, asking T-Man yet another inane question, but as she left the building Louise heard nothing but silence from behind her.

She took a taxi back to Crystal House. The driver complimented her on her costume. He even knew who she was.

'Great weather, huh, Miss Bale?' he said. 'I had a choice. Either go to the festival, or to go to work and then go straight on down to the beach. I know you'll not be upset to hear I chose work, and I'm going to the beach later, but I do follow your Superhero doings, and it's great to have the festival in Crescent City. Hey, is it true that the big guy, you know, *T-Man,* is in town?'

'Yes, T-Man's here. I've just seen him.'

As the door to Crystal House rolled shut behind her and the bolts rammed home, Louise felt relieved to be back, even with Jeff still here in the house. He couldn't harm her any more in his present state. She wondered idly if he was still OK, or if she really ought to have called an ambulance for him.

She could not hear Jeff, but trusted that the house defences would protect her against anything he might do. She began to relax, thinking that she was safe now. The house would protect her from both Jeff and Conway Johns.

But then, with a frightening tingle of pain around her scalp, she realised that her logic was faulty. The defences of Crystal House were not truly hers, because Conway Johns was the one who had built them.

Exeter sat on the canvas seat in the military transport plane. At last, he had escaped from the South, having found that his sister was safe. He still hadn't been able to get his message out to Louise, but he would contact her as soon as the plane landed. He looked at the clouds outside the tiny window and imagined what it would be like if he could be a Superhero, flying without the aid of this aeroplane, this massive oil-powered artificial structure. But even then, he thought, he would not feel the freedom that he felt now.

Chapter Forty-One

As Louise went upstairs to find Jeff, she wondered again whether it had been a mistake for her to return to Crystal House. Being threatened by Jeff was bad enough, but what about Conway Johns? And what was happening right now back at the convention hall? She began to wonder ominously if anyone back there would survive. She went to her bedroom, expecting Jeff to still be in her bed, but he was not.

'Jeff?'

She wondered if the house might have killed him and hidden his body away.

'Jeff?'

She went through to the kitchen, then she went out to the landing in the main part of the house.

'Jeff?' she called out for the third time. Then she caught sight of herself in the gleaming side of one of the silver women. She was beautiful in the Moon Queen costume.

She went to the Moon Room and looked out at the trees. She looked at their sickness and remembered that she had never found out what it was that caused that. Then a footstep came behind her.

'Hey, Louise!'

It was Jeff. He was up and walking. He stood in the doorway with one arm behind his back. Louise smiled uneasily, and Jeff grinned too, but he still kept that one arm behind him.

'Hi, Jeff,' Louise said. 'What's in your other hand?'

Jeff looked confused for a second but then brought the hidden hand forward. It held a kitchen knife. This was so crazy that Louise nearly laughed.

'What are you doing with that?'

Jeff stared at the knife and then at Louise, as if making up his mind what to do.

'I felt nervous on my own, in the house,' he said, and made as if to lay the knife down on the floor, but he did it very slowly and kept staring at her.

'Why are you not coming towards me, Louise?' he asked. 'Don't you love me? Why aren't you coming over here to kiss me? Surely you're not scared?'

Still stooped down, he began examining the knife closely, touching it with his thumb, as if testing the sharpness of the blade. He stood up, then ran forward and lunged at Louise. She jumped back and scrambled away behind the Moon Chair. Jeff came up on the other side, lunging with the knife. Which way would he go? Which way round the chair would he go when he tried to rush her? Or would he wait, wait for her to get scared, and then kill her when she made a run for it?

She was about to take a step backwards, away from the Chair, when she saw that it would be a bad move. She would be cornered then, with her back to the wall. So she darted forward to the left of the Chair. She had no time to check Jeff's reactions, she just had to trust her luck.

It worked. She'd sent him the wrong way. She ran for the doorway, out into the corridor, to the front door. But, despite being slowed by the wounds to his legs and rear, Jeff was right behind her.

'*House, save me!*' Louise shouted, trying to make the house spring its traps, but the house did nothing. Her words stopped Jeff though.

'I *knew* it was you that did it,' he said. 'You made this house microwave me. You made it grind me in that chair. I'm going to come after you slowly, Louise, checking for your clever little traps. And when I get to you, you're going to pay for what you've done to me.'

He came cautiously forward with the knife, still checking from side to side as he advanced towards her. Louise, still facing him, scrabbled her hands around the cape at her back and began to work at the bolts of the door behind her. She heard them unlatching, and then heard the door roll open.

But when Louise turned to run, she was met by a cloud of steam and a roar of flame. Crystal House had a visitor waiting outside. Morthwil was standing there.

Chapter Forty-Two

Morthwil stood outside the front door. Flames raged from his hands, and wisps of steam issued from vents on his legs. He looked even more terrible than he had on TV, on the day he'd destroyed Conway Johns' - his own - house. He now no longer looked anything like T-Man. Louise began to hear distant sirens from the town, as if something terrible had happened down there. Behind her, she saw that Jeff had collapsed to the floor and was trying to edge away.

Morthwil had been staring up at the structure of the house, not at Louise, but now his eyes moved to look down at her. The fire from his hands ceased, but more steam issued from the vents in his legs, and then, suddenly, he began to grow, as if he was now so far beyond being human that he could even change his size at will. He was growing, inflating, becoming more massive and more dangerous by the second. The steam blasts became stronger, as if it took vast amounts of energy for Morthwil to increase his size.

And then Louise felt the whole structure of Crystal House begin to shake. Shutters slammed across the windows, inside and out, and then flaps above the windows clunked open to dump concrete into the gaps. The front door began to roll shut. It looked as if the house was going to protect Louise after all. But then, to her horror, a third arm suddenly unfolded from Morthwil's front and telescoped up to a peculiar socket that had just opened up on the front of the house. The third arm rotated slightly, and Louise saw that a thick cable now connected Morthwil to the house. The door stopped rolling shut and opened again.

Crystal House gradually became silent, as if Morthwil had stifled all its defences. There was a crumbling sound, and Louise felt herself tilting backwards as the doorstep cracked in two beneath her foot and gave way to a hole in the ground. She fell into blackness.

The sky was sullen and the Young Master was bored. No, not bored. He was lacking in something. There was something that had to happen, but he did not know what. Then there came a movement behind him. AM-12 stood by the door.

'Sir,' AM-12 ventured. 'Is it the hour?'

The Young Master inclined his head towards the robot. He knew what AM-12 meant. He would go with the faithful machine and let it lead him to the outbuildings, to the machinery there, where his reawakening would take place.

Louise awoke in terrible pain and knew that her back was broken. She was either blind or in the darkness of some cavity beneath Crystal House.

Then a faint light came from somewhere above her, just out of sight, but she could not move her head to look. She saw stars, but the stars were all black. Perhaps, she thought, that meant she was about to die.

Then she saw that the stars were flies. She felt them landing on her body, walking over her costume and her skin, but she was in too much pain to swat them off. She felt the flies crawling to and from the smashed section of her back.

Then the sensation became soothing, as if the insects were anaesthetising her, and she felt as if someone was blowing gently into her face. She opened her eyes and saw a number of the flies hovering in front of her like tiny little aeroplanes, lightly pushing the air forward. She felt more filthy with every second, but also more reassembled inside. She could move her feet and toes again.

She tried moving her arms, head, and legs, found she could now move them without pain, and climbed cautiously up to the lip of the broken-open hole where she had fallen by the front door. She felt her spine moving easily again. She poked her head out and, with a shock, saw that Morthwil was still standing there. He was looking the other way, but by now he had to be thirty feet tall. He had disconnected himself from Crystal House. Louise sprang out from the hole onto the blackened grass. Little fires burnt everywhere and the air was hot.

Then she saw that sections of the house were slowly moving. The house was collapsing in a specially-ordered way, its walls sliding quietly down in sequence into prepared slots in the ground, as if there would soon be nothing left of it but the Moon Chair, standing alone among a series of low walls. Louise thought of turning to run, but she did not because that was not why she had been healed.

She took one step towards the Morthwil, the monster, then another. A fierce heat radiated from him. Despite her healing, she must not make the mistake of thinking she was invulnerable now. Morthwil swung very slowly from side to side. The transformation from the big man who had bullied Louise at the festival to this enormous monster was the strangest thing she had ever known. As she approached, she saw what looked like a maintenance ladder leading up one of Morthwil's steaming legs. Some flies accompanied her as she ran forward, grabbed the rungs, and began to climb. She used her cape to help shield the flies from the heat; they had helped her and so they deserved that.

When Morthwil noticed that Louise was climbing his leg, he began swaying violently, trying to dislodge her. She looked down and, on the terrible whirling ground beneath, saw Jeff lying on the grass. The branches of a tree swung towards her and she had to scramble around to the other side of the ladder as the twigs and leaves slashed past. Louise looked up and saw where the ladder led into what looked like an access chamber in the monster above her. The angles of Morthwil's legs as he whirled around meant that the entrance to the chamber opened and shut. Louise had to time it just right to climb up there, in between swings, but the flies encouraged her. She felt them land on her arms and legs, as if trying to guide her, like tiny riders on a giant horse. They had the timing. The space swung open, then shut, then open again. At the right instant, they urged her on. She made her move. And then she was inside the monster.

The flies swirled around a hatch that was now above her head, showing her which way to turn the lever to open it, and then she ascended into the whirling monster. Inside was an almost circular room that contained several large mechanical objects. The hatch dropped back shut behind her. She saw what looked like a trough of acid in which shapes were being dissolved. The acid vapour made the bare parts of her flesh and her eyes sting, but the flies were even worse affected. They soon fell to the floor, their wings etched through.

Louise looked back at the closed hatch from where she had come, barely able to see it now because her eyes stung so much. She moved back towards it but had to close her eyes and so lost her way. She fumbled around for a few seconds and bumped into one of the walls. Forcing her eyes open again, she saw a kind of torpedo tube mounted there, but inside the tube was what looked like a dead body. In fantastic, morbid curiosity, Louise touched the body through a hole in the side of the tube, but it felt dried-up, corrupted, and rotten.

She found a window in the wall from where she could see out. She saw the ground, still swinging around below, and then she saw Exeter down there. He had come home. Her vision was blurring into a curtain of redness as her face began to bleed, but she saw Theo down there too.

Chapter Forty-Three

Through the smeary red haze of blood, Louise looked out from the window in Morthwil's belly and saw Exeter and Theo down on the grass below. Theo looked older now, as if he had been changed in some way. He was carrying a hunting rifle, custom-made for his child's body. Then Theo spotted Louise's face looking down at them. He grabbed Exeter's arm and pointed up at her. Theo ran up close to Morthwil and took aim even as Louise tried to wave him away. Morthwil swung around, as if he had not yet noticed either Theo or Exeter, and Louise saw Crystal House again. It had collapsed right down - all that was left was the Moon Chair and the silver women.

Then Louise heard Theo's gun fire. The bullet bounced off Morthwil's armour with a deep, hollow clang. She felt Morthwil's huge body stop mid-swing, adjusting its intentions, as if he had now noticed the two people below.

The body structure creaked as Morthwil raised his massive fist. The window turned towards Theo, but he leapt out of the way just as the fist pounded into the ground where he had been standing. Louise was jarred by the concussion. Theo and Exeter sprinted away, and Morthwil paused, apparently having decided they were not worth the chase.

But Theo had not gone far. He returned, having just run around Morthwil in a great circle, and now approached his massive feet from behind. But then he just stood there, looking up at him, as if he had run out of inspiration for what to do next. Louise heard Exeter calling to Theo from somewhere out of sight.

Morthwil's swinging motion began again as he saw that Theo had returned. Louise screamed at Theo to get away because he was powerless against a being so many times his size.

A powerful roaring began. Squinting through a fresh run of blood in her eyes, Louise saw a stream of fire blaze down and nearly hit Theo right in the face.

The silver women, who had been standing amid what remained of Crystal House, began to move. Their eyes glowed red as they ran to protect Theo with incredible speed. One of them scooped Theo up and began to carry him away, even as he struggled to get free, while the others came right up to Morthwil and began to clamp themselves around his legs. One of them went behind and managed to unbalance him somehow, because Louise felt the monster start to tip over. It all happened very quickly. The ground swung up towards her, and she slid forwards onto the window - now beneath her - as Morthwil fell. It felt to Louise as if the whole earth shook, but the mechanical objects inside him, even the trough of acid and the torpedo tube, simply pivoted on giant gyroscopic mounts.

Morthwil's body shuddered and shrieked as he raised himself again to his feet. He stood differently now, with his legs further apart, as if he had learned from the silver women's attack. Through the window, Louise saw his hand grab at one of the women by her head and legs. He tore her apart and flung the pieces away. The rest of the women came forward to attack, but they had no tricks left. Morthwil grabbed them and broke them apart one by one.

Then Louise saw Theo again. He had got free of the silver woman who had rescued him and was coming back. She could hear his shouts.

'Miss Bale! Miss Bale!'

Morthwil lurched towards Theo with incredible speed and knocked him down with his huge fist.

Morthwil came to a stop, standing by where Theo lay, and Louise saw a picture appear on a wall inside the monster, like an old film. It showed Theo and another small boy playing as children. The other boy was showing off by lifting up a big rock while Theo watched in amazement. The other boy laughed, but then his laughter changed to a cry of fear when he put the boulder down and saw that his arms had started to wither away.

The picture vanished. Louise wiped more blood from her eyes and looked outside the window again. Morthwil stepped forward slowly. Louise could see exactly what was going to happen but was powerless to stop it. She saw Exeter running to save Theo, but he could not possibly be quick enough. Morthwil stepped forward and crushed Theo's body into the ground with his huge foot. Then there was silence.

Morthwil slowly ticked round on his axis. There was a whirring noise and the sound of something slipping, and Louise saw the rotten human body she had seen in its torpedo tube fall from Morthwil's front and slump onto the ground beneath. It was the body of Hyperion.

Louise looked at the pathetic crumpled form on the grass and remembered the times Hyperion had disguised himself and come to Crystal House just because he had loved her aunt.

Out of the window, Louise now saw that something had changed about the Moon Chair. Behind the seat, a tiny door had opened in its back. Morthwil stood still, watching, as the door folded into itself. And then, through the misty red blur, Louise saw something incredible. She saw *herself* crawling out from inside the back of the chair. How could that be? But then she realised what was happening. The caped figure crawling out of the chair was more graceful and fine-featured than she ever could be. She was seeing her aunt, Agnes Bale, the real Moon Queen.

From all around her, Louise heard Morthwil's voice speak.

'Agnes!' it said.

'You may have taken control of Crystal House,' the Moon Queen said, 'but you will never control me!'

'Ever since I became T-Man,' Morthwil said, 'I loved you, and you knew that. From the first time I ever used my powers, you have always been within my mind. You must love me. You must respond. I created Morthwil that I might fight him, so that you would love me for defending you.'

'I never did love you, Conway. Nothing you could ever do could make me love you. I remember how you tried to make me grateful after you built my defences here.'

Louise saw another scene, like another old film, appear on the wall inside Morthwil. Conway Johns and the Moon Queen were inside Crystal House, and Johns was explaining to her how to use an elaborate control panel. As the Moon Queen moved her hand to one of the switches, Johns leaned forward to touch her.

She turned on him angrily, and his face filled with fury.

'I knew that you created Morthwil,' the Moon Queen said, as the old memory played.

Another image formed inside Morthwil's body. Louise saw Hyperion in jail, with the Moon Queen lecturing him through the bars. Hyperion said something that made the Moon Queen laugh, and then she reached in and stroked Hyperion's cheek. Then Louise saw Conway Johns alone, starting work on a terrible new project, building a new costume of armour, to become Morthwil.

'After Morthwil disappeared years ago I thought that was an end to it,' the Moon Queen said. 'But then I heard that Morthwil had come back to the world again. It was when you damaged your own house, pretending you had been attacked. So I pretended to die, to leave the world, in the hope that you would not think about me anymore.

'I listened in to your speech at the festival today, Conway. I heard you say that puny humans had to be rescued from their own mistakes. What about *your* mistakes? You were mistaken that I could ever love you. You killed the Golden Man and you killed Glinda.'

Louise saw a further scene inside the monster. She saw huge hammer hands burst from the clouds and smash into the Golden Man and Glinda as they flew by.

'I always knew you were evil. You goaded the Lead Coffin into new attacks. You killed Hyperion. You yourself deserve to die, Conway.'

A white ray shot out from the Moon Chair, and Morthwil's whole body shook. Searing white flames covered the outside of the glass. Then Louise saw Jeff. He was standing up and had found the knife. The old Moon Queen was still blasting at Morthwil and did not see Jeff approach her. Louise screamed at her aunt to look out, but then, almost lazily, Jeff sank his knife deep into Agnes Bale's back and wrenched it out to stab again. The old Moon Queen dropped her weapon and fell down. Morthwil's whole body shook, and with a terrible roar, he ran forward.

Louise's eyes were flooded with blood again. She was blinded for a few seconds until she saw Jeff wrestling with Exeter. Exeter had got the knife from him and pulled Jeff aside as Morthwil's great hands grabbed the Moon Queen's body. The hands lifted the body gently, raising it slowly up to the window, and squeezed it grotesquely against the glass. Morthwil was clutching the old Moon Queen to himself in grief. A terrible wailing came from Morthwil's whole structure as Louise stared at her aunt's beautiful dead face through the window.

And then the body was dropped. It fell to the ground with a distant thump.

Louise saw Jeff standing there, frozen in fear as Morthwil advanced on him. Jeff looked up and saw Louise inside Morthwil. She saw his lips move, crying out for her to forgive him. But then Morthwil grabbed Jeff by his head and his legs, lifted him from the ground, and, jerkily and slowly, tore him in half.

Louise felt a terrible satisfaction as Morthwil threw Jeff away, out of sight, in two different directions. The earth did not shake as Jeff's halves landed.

'I remember that man,' Morthwil said. 'He asked to meet me. I thought he saw my other life. I thought he saw through my deception.'

Chapter Forty-Four

Morthwil knelt by the Moon Chair amid the folded-down walls of Crystal House. His giant hands spread into fingers that picked at the little door in the back of the Chair. Inside there was a tiny cabin, like the inside of a doll's house. There was a little seat next to a control panel, a store of food, and a miniature toilet. Agnes Bale had been hiding inside the Moon Chair all the time.

Morthwil re-made his fists, swung his hammer-hands, and smashed the Moon Chair aside. Then he turned back around. Louise saw Theo returning to life and Exeter helping him up from where he had been crushed into the ground. Morthwil lurched towards them.

Louise had forced herself to keep her eyes open, but now the pain became too much. She explored the cavity inside Morthwil with her hands, making sure she avoided the acid vat, until she came to something soft. It was something that had just descended into the room. It felt like a human head.

She opened her eyes again and found she was looking into Conway Johns' face. The head was not attached to a body, but rested on a spherical stand where it was attached by wires and tubes. That was how he had changed his size, how he could be both Morthwil and T-Man at the same time. He had no real human body. This was how the problem of his body wasting away when he used his special strength had been solved.

'It is time for you to die, you who are within me,' the head said, swivelling on its stand to look at Louise. A surge of bubbles began to rise from the acid vat, and another steaming cloud of vapour began to fill the room. The head started to be lifted upwards again, out of range of the acid.

Louise slammed her eyes shut again as she grabbed at Conway Johns' head and tried to wrench it from its stand. The choking vapour burned her face and hands. Then she raised her foot high and kicked into the head as hard as she could. She slipped and fell to the floor, but she had felt something give. The head had been kicked to one side but was still connected to the stand by the wires. Louise grabbed at it again, gripping it now inside her elbow, tight against the side of her body. She twisted at it, trying to kill it, to force her fingers into its eyes, as the huge bodywork of the room rolled and bucked around her. Then, as she pulled and twisted at the skull, a core of wires and ligaments finally tore out from inside.

The whole room screamed. She had almost dragged the head right across to the acid trough now. She gave a final, savage heave, felt the last of the wires rip free, and then she plunged the head into the acid.

The outside whirled around the window. Louise saw the ground and then the sky. Then she saw the remains of Crystal House, which was trying to rise again, trying to rebuild itself. Some of the walls around the Moon Room were attempting to lift themselves back up and slot back into place, but the process was not working properly. Wet concrete began pouring from hidden ducts but just piled up in formless mounds.

Louise was alone in a world of fire. The acid was inside her costume now, running down her arms, burning. The monster outside slammed into the ground, face down, and the window went black.

Louise awoke to see Exeter's face amid a cloud of flies. He had his arm around her.

'I got you out,' he said. Theo was behind him. He was standing and beginning to look normal again, because he was the Die Master and could never be killed. He came and placed his hands onto Louise's eyes. She felt her vision clear. He put his hands onto her scalp, and she felt healing there too. All her wounds were mending - even the changes the flies had made were being cleansed from her body.

'Heal my aunt,' Louise said, but she saw that the Moon Queen's body was gone.

Theo offered to mend Jeff too, but Louise shook her head.

'No. I don't want him back.'

Theo turned away from them and said he needed to return home. He said it was time to forget.

Chapter Forty-Five

Louise remained in Crescent City for several weeks and stayed at the Peacock Motel. A lot of international attention was now focused on Crescent City, and she began to have to avoid interviewers. Exeter made sure she was always able to get away.

After Louise had left the Superhero Festival, T-Man had killed Joe and Carl for mocking him. It was all on video, clearly visible - the moment when the looks on their faces changed from complacency to fear. After their deaths, T-Man had begun to mutate into Morthwil in front of everyone's eyes. Larry Chill, Captain Z, and the Tribune had tried to reason with him but barely escaped with their lives.

The threat from the Oil Lands to the south had gone. Following the destruction of Morthwil, they had given up. All their oil belonged to President Rayonier now.

One evening, while Exeter was busy at the motel, Louise went up to the site of Crystal House. The remains of Morthwil had been taken away by heavy machinery over the past few weeks. She passed the awful ruined shell of the house, still half risen from the ground and flooded with a solid flow of concrete, and remembered how the flies had healed her in a hole beneath there. She found the sickly pool where the flies lived and stared at its putrefaction.

She went on through the grounds until she reached the edge of a cliff where the trees ended. She could see all of Crescent City from here. The wind blew over the fresh new hair growing on her scalp, and she remembered how Theo had healed her. He would be back at home among his remaining robots, again living his happy life as a child.

Louise continued along the clifftop. This was a corner of these grounds she had never explored, a place that was higher than the rest of the garden. It was a good hill for the flies, which buzzed around her face. There had to be something up here for them. She wondered what it was.

She was about to return to the Peacock Motel when she saw something in the grass a little way off. It looked like two logs, severely eroded by the weather. But the flies seemed to love them. They buzzed around the logs in thick clouds. Louise went closer, and then stopped, because now she could see what the logs really were.

'Thank you, Hyperion,' Louise said. 'Thank you for sending your flies to heal me in that hole and get me inside Morthwil. And thank you, Aunt Agnes, for looking after me in Crystal House.'

The logs were the decayed remains of two human bodies. The Moon Queen and Hyperion lay in the open, with flies travelling in almost solid lines between them and the trees. Louise felt tears come as she wondered what her aunt felt now. She wondered if her aunt could now go down the hill from where her body lay and, free of the lust of others, be alone with Hyperion at last - if they could now fly all over the hill together and see it through thousands of tiny eyes.

THE END